St Ives Unframed

The 1960s

One Off! A Magical Era

Christine Farrington

Published by New Generation Publishing in 2019

Copyright © Christine Farrington 2019

First Edition

The author asserts the moral right under the Copyright, Designs and Patents Act 1988 to be identified as the author of this work.

All Rights reserved. No part of this publication may be reproduced, stored in a retrieval system or transmitted, in any form or by any means without the prior consent of the author, nor be otherwise circulated in any form of binding or cover other than that which it is published and without a similar condition being imposed on the subsequent purchaser.

ISBN: 978-1-78955-770-1

www.newgeneration-publishing.com
New Generation Publishing

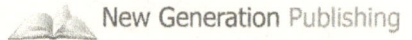

For Carol Jackson with Love

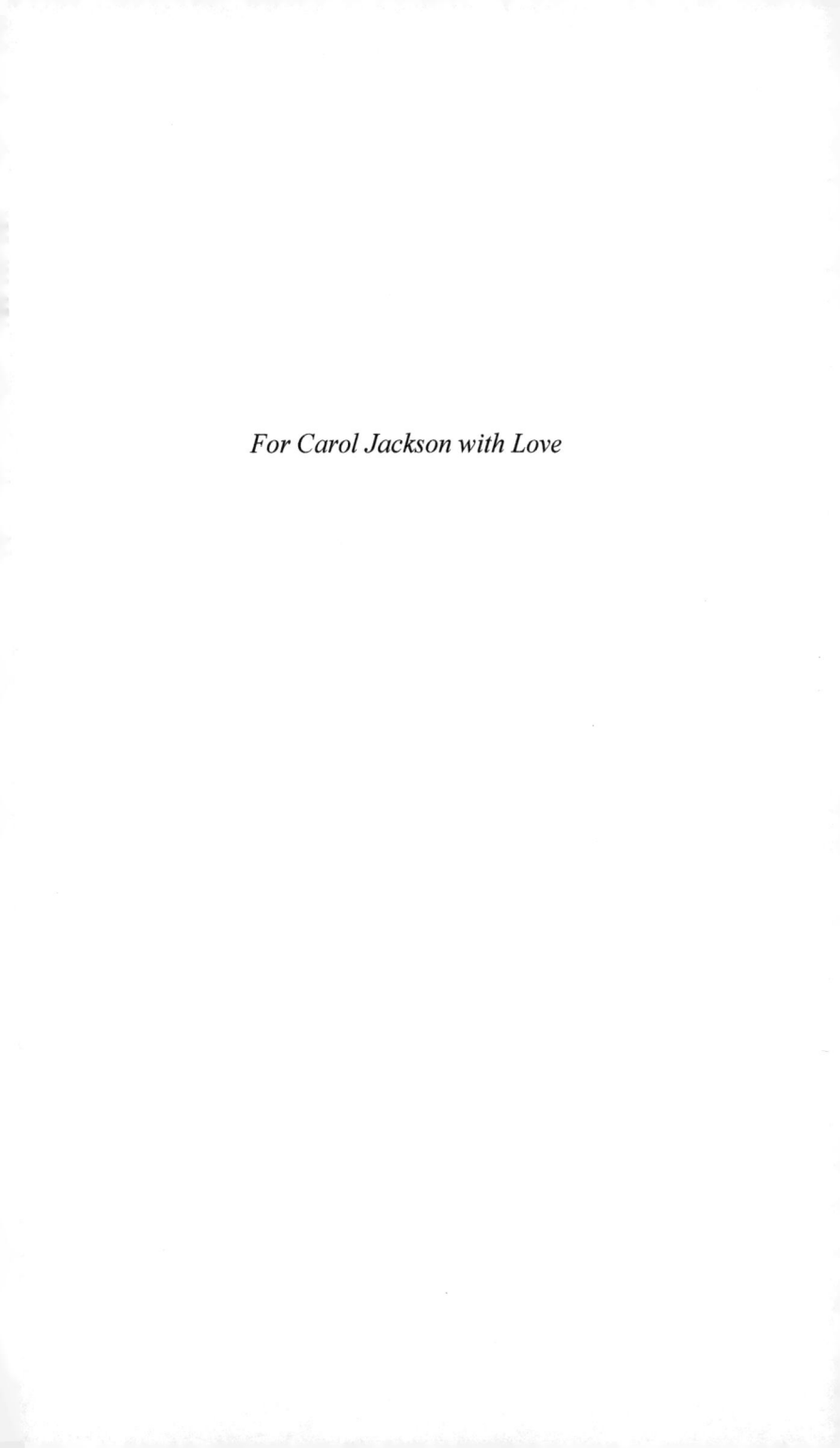

St Ives

Even in the falling light St Ives has a luminous quality. Facing north, but surrounded on three sides by the Atlantic, the town bathes in a high level of ultra-violet light reflected from the sea, giving the painted houses a shimmering unreality, even at dusk. Bernard Leach set up a pottery here in 1920, still in production now, followed by Barbara Hepworth and her giant sculptures. The light attracted artists from all over the world and the little fishing village became a colony of bohemian life. Then the tourists came, then the Tate St Ives Art Gallery, then more tourists, then the pilchards left and the town's fate was sealed.

Chapter One

St Ives 2018

"It's Museum of the Year" stated The Cornishman proudly in its Thursday, July 12th, 2018 edition. Posters and banners heralding that St Ives's national treasure, the Tate St Ives Museum, has won this prestigious award with a whopping prize of one hundred thousand pounds and the "incredible honour" of being named Museum of the Year. This was indeed good news, and I for one couldn't wait to visit the Tate whilst on a three month sabbatical in the beautiful Cornish town with its myriad of stunning beaches, art galleries, potteries, craft shops, surf shops, pasties, and cream teas. Above all, it's the light. St Ives with that brilliant light that has attracted and brought so many artists for years and years from all over the world, to paint in the Jewel of the Cornish Crown.

By mere chance, I had happened upon a brief notice on Facebook, a lady advertising a small, noisy flat in central St Ives to rent. Earplugs might be needed she stated in the description, especially on Sundays when the nearby St Ives Parish Church bells would be calling its flock to early morning prayer. The flat was situated above a busy restaurant that functioned from 9 a.m. until 10 p.m. every day in the summer months and might create further noise. There would be a view of the nearby harbour from the front bedroom window if only the church would cut away some of their overhanging trees – it used to be so nice to see the sea, she stated! Not one of these things put me off, especially for the three peak holiday months – the kind lady offered me a reduced rental that made the long visit to my beloved St Ives possible. Something in the region of £10,000 difference than any other rental being charged for the same time and period . . . how lucky was that! I think it was the quirkiness of the description of the flat and the rather obscure pictures she sent via email together with her complete honesty of noise, earplugs, obliterated view of the sea that clinched the deal.

The booking of the flat had taken place the previous November, so I had plenty of time to get my life in order. I was living in Cape Town, 6000 miles away in a house with views of rolling hills, fields, horses and springbok, a lovely river and above all, perfect peace. It was hard to get a picture of what life was going to be like living in St Ives for three months, full of noise, a mass of people thronging the narrow streets and crowding the beautiful beaches. If I wanted to be in Cornwall in the warm weather then I had to take what went with it, otherwise, my stay there would have had to be in quieter and colder months.

For the first time in about fifty years, I was without a car. I'd decided that the cost of hiring a car for three months would be madness and the restriction of little parking in St Ives made it a no brainer, so I duly sent for a Senior Railcard – this proved to be a great novelty and one which appealed to me enormously. Public transport in the UK, both rail and bus services, were great. So much easier having someone else do the driving while as a passenger you could read, listen to music or send off those all-important emails or simply gaze out of the window at the passing scenery. From London's Heathrow Airport to St Ives' picturesque railway station took approximately 5hr 22mins and I couldn't have enjoyed it more. No queuing for a rental car, then battling to get out of London and ending up in interminable roadworks or traffic jams. No, public transport was the way to go, and I loved every minute of it.

That momentous time, fifty-five years back, when I'd first visited St Ives in 1963, still filled me with wondrous joy at seeing the harbour and Porthminster beach as the little train trundled into the station. Being born and bred in the industrial north of England, surrounded by cotton mills and back-to-back houses, it was hard to imagine that anywhere as quaint, sunny, and warm existed on the same planet. Arriving in 2018 by a smarter, faster train to a station slightly more modernised and clean with car parking and taxis surrounding it in perpetual motion made not the slightest difference – it was beloved St Ives with the scent of the Atlantic Ocean lapping onto the long sandy beaches, its palm trees and blue, blue sky that has captivated and attracted tourists in their droves for the last half-century.

Relieved to have finally arrived at my destination after such a long journey, I trundled my two medium wheelie suitcases up from the station to Pedn Olva steps that lead down into The Warren – this was not an easy task, one wheelie is bad enough, but two was like . . . out of control. Old age does have its compensations, and several kindly gentlemen offered to carry the cases down the steep flight of steps for me – thank you. It would be downhill all the way from there. Even still, steering the two wheelie's downhill was almost as bad as dragging them uphill, leaving me totally uncoordinated and slightly out of control. *Did I really need all these clothes*? I kept mumbling to myself.

Down The Warren, past the Arts Club and left into St Andrews Street, up to St Ives Parish Church and there was the Market Place. I was to meet Sarah, the cleaning and changeover lady, who would be waiting at the rear of the building to show me the flat and hand over the keys – and there she was as arranged, with a bright, welcoming smile and strong arms to relieve me of my cases. The building seemed old, and the interior fell short of the 1950s with an air of bedsitter-land of the same period. A couple of flights of stone staircases and dark landings later, we reached the flat door, and Sarah let us in. Two double bedrooms, a smaller than small shower room and toilet, a sitting-room cum kitchen with two superb sash windows, one looking out over the Market Place and the other across at the ancient granite walls of the Market House with pretty troughs full of blossoming flowers on the sash window ledges and a granite stone marking its date, 1832. The front bedroom also boasted a large sash window looking over the Market Place to Fore Street and down towards the lifeboat house and the harbour a stone's throw away. The second double bedroom was at the rear and away from the buzz of the Market Place; it was slightly larger than the front bedroom. I was pleasantly delighted with the quirky flat with its myriad of colours. It was small, compact and everything that I could possibly need to make my three months stay in St Ives . . . perfect.

After Sarah left, I looked around the flat and luxuriated in my good fortune at having discovered such a place. Choosing the green rear bedroom to sleep in, I dumped my cases and went out to do some shopping. It was Sunday and St Ives was alive even at 5 p.m. The High Street and Tregenna Place shops were still open to my delight and relief. I stocked up with the essentials at the Co-op store that had everything anyone could possibly need. I discovered the butcher, the bakers, and Boots the Chemist were all literally . . . on my doorstep. The smells permeating from the different shops were inviting. Pasties, warm crusty baguettes, and scones for the cream teas as well as freshly-ground coffee wafting out of the café doorways, was wonderful. Back at the flat, I prepared a plate of Brie and Camembert with some juicy black grapes and poured myself a large glass of Pinot Grigio . . . delicious. Utterly replete and happy with the excitement of it all, I promptly fell asleep for the next eleven hours.

Something rumbling along like the noise of tanks woke me up the following morning and it appeared to be outside and underneath the long narrow bedroom window – curiosity got the better of me and I leapt out of bed and drew back the white muslin curtain to discover what looked like a rather large street cleaning machine spraying out water with four massive circular brushes sweeping the streets of St Ives clean for the oncoming day. Following that, another big truck, but this time it was to collect the weekend's tonnage of empty bottles from the three nearby pubs – there would be no getting away from this particular noise. I was soon to learn that the cleaning and collecting took place before the town woke up and the tourists began their search for the best breakfast places, as shopkeepers began the arduous task of opening up and getting their goods out on display.

    Feeling completely refreshed and as early as it was, I slipped on a pair of shorts, t-shirt, my Reef flip-flops and headed down to West Pier and the harbour. The tide was high, so no walking across the Harbour Beach and plunging into the sea in a flurry of freedom, which is exactly what I wanted to do. Instead, I took a stroll along the harbour front, taking in the smells and feeling the town come to life. Everything appeared exactly as I left it those many years ago, yet, everything was different. A new lifeboat house now stood at the start of West Pier with the RNLI tourist shop next to it. The old lifeboat house was now a smart-looking restaurant. Thereafter each building had become something else, catering for the resurgence of St Ives in the advent of such fame as the Rosamunde Pilcher books and the TV Series made from them, each with a St Ives and Cornwall theme. Then followed the Tate St Ives that opened its doors in 1993 on the site of the old gasworks overlooking Porthmeor Beach and the Atlantic Ocean – in the first six months it welcomed over 120,000 visitors – 50,000 more than the original target for the entire year. Then the latter-day and hugely successful TV series of Poldark from the novels of Winston Graham who wrote his first Poldark novel in 1945, subsequently eleven more followed ending with "Bella" in 2002. So, it was little wonder that every type of restaurant existed to cater for the eclectic holidaymakers heading to St Ives because of its beautiful beaches, good surfing, fine weather, the artist colony, and its many art galleries, and now the Tate St Ives Museum. Luckily for me, the pasty outlets appeared to have quadrupled in numbers along the front, and fish and chips were still to be had in quite a few more places than I remembered.

It was wonderful to be in the throng of everything as the town awoke on Monday morning, a whole new start to another week, new visitors to cater for and to attract into the many packed gift shops that lined the harbour front and the very busy and narrow Fore Street that ran parallel behind it. By mid-morning the place was buzzing with people, lorries unloading goods, catering vans delivering food, refrigerated ice-cream vans stocking up, Warrens Bakery filling their many outlets with pasties, sausage rolls, bread, scones and cakes galore. It was good to see a landmark of the past, Harbour Amusement and Pool Club still going strong and fairly unaltered, although it now boasted a restaurant above it next to the pool room that commanded a superb view across the harbour. The Sloop Inn already had people sitting outside eating breakfast, and I noticed the odd surreptitious pint of beer being drunk at that hour in the morning. What the hell, people were on holiday. Taking in everything at once was pretty mind-boggling so, armed with a warm sausage roll, I made my way back to the flat.

That afternoon, low tide would be at 2.39 p.m. and I did not want to miss being out there at that time. I stuffed my shorts pockets with iPhone, money, keys, and an old sail tie for attaching my slip-flops to when I was on the beach. Taking the slipway at West Pier – a mere 50 meters from the flat – I decided to walk straight over to the shoreline at the end of Smeaton's Pier. The water was beautiful, clear, cold and refreshing, and the tide well out. The rocks surrounding Pedn Olver Hotel to the right were completely clear of the water at such low tide, and instinctively I was drawn to walking across this stretch of the harbour beach rounding Pedn Olver rocks and onto Porthminster Beach walking through the water and the waves until I could go no further. Feeling exhilarated and not wanting this to end, I turned around and walked all the way back again, this time taking in the small spit of sand left between Smeaton's Pier and the incoming tide which I managed to do before it was too late. Leaping onto what is left of the old wooden pier, up some steps which brings you out to the start of Smeaton's Pier at Quay Street. That first good couple of miles walking through the clear, blue water, that gave me such pleasure, set precedence for the rest of my stay in St Ives.

Having two loves in one's life, Cornwall and Africa, and with the reality of advancing years, it became a consuming desire to spend, after thirty-three years in Africa, some period of time in Cornwall and especially in St Ives, to see and experience for myself, what it would be like to live in England again should it first, become necessary and secondly, if my heart was still here. Basically, I call it a spiritual journey, a Camino de St Ives. To do plenty of barefoot walking along the beaches following the coastline, swimming, lots of reading, and studying philosophy. Above all, it was a time to be alone to think and to reflect.

In the early '60s and '70s when I first visited and consequently lived in St Ives, it was at a time in life that was young, exciting, and carefree. People escaping large cities, seeking an alternative life, flocked to Cornwall where beatniks, hippies and flower power groups were descending in droves. Dreary people, colourful people, artists, potters, musicians, and poets fell for the charm, the sun, the beaches and the dramatic rocky coastline of the beautiful area with its special light nestling on the South Western tip of England. It was a wonderful time for me where I made many friends, worked in the hospitality trade, signed on the dole, learned new skills, and ultimately became a jeweller. But did I know St Ives? No, not one little jot. Just arrived there, stepped onto the social roundabout of work, socialising in The Sloop Inn, flower picking in the winter, driving out to Zennor for lunch at The Tinner's Arms on a Sunday, seemed to fill my time. As far as discovering St Ives itself – I simply went around with my eyes tight shut.

So re-discovering St Ives was high on my list on this special visit. I would walk the town taking in every street, pathway, alleyway, the countless amounts of steps, hills, and back roads until I knew it, like I wanted so much to know, this little piece of paradise. So I set out a plan to walk every day as part of my exercise, making half the walk along the beach at low tide, and the other half through the town.

And awakened, I soon became. Donning shorts, a t-shirt, and flip-flops and after studying the tide table, I set out each day with wallet and iPhone in a bum bag strapped across my back and sallied forth. Grabbing a sausage roll or a small pasty before heading down the West Pier slipway and onto the large stretch of the Harbour Beach where I took off my flip-flops and tied them with a lanyard hooked onto the bum bag, heading towards the shoreline taking a right turn once I'd hit the water. I loved walking around the rocks – where the Pedn Olva Hotel perched precariously on top – these were only accessible during a short period between high and low tides. With the sand beneath my feet in the cold Atlantic water, feeling energised, exhilarated, and happy, my whole being took on a different persona.

In the yesteryears, there is no recollection of Porthminster Beach ever being part of our lifestyle. It was certainly not the "In" beach to hang out on. The harbour or Porthmeor beaches were the infra-dig places to be seen, more especially Porthmeor for the surfing and a lovely collection of Australian surf-lifesavers. Porthminster was strictly for the up-country tourists. Now I find myself gravitating towards Porthminster with its crescent of golden sand framed by a glittering bay with glorious views across to Godrevy Lighthouse. This is truly a wonderful beach for swimming, paddle-boarding, canoeing, or merely just walking through the waves or across the sand. Depending on the tide, I would take the steps leading off Porthminster by the mini-golf course and up past the Pedn Olva Hotel and back down The Warren where I re-discovered St Ives Arts Club, and where I met my old friend, Bob Devereaux.

With the arrival of the railway in 1877, Cornwall, especially St Ives with its clear light became a mecca for artists and in 1890 the St Ives Arts Club was founded around a cricket table which is still in the foyer. The minute books, since 1890 are still kept at the club. Today's membership includes anyone who is interested in the club, its main activities being music, drama, and painting, as well as social events. It boasts a charming little theatre where poets, musicians, singers, and Bob Devereaux, poet, performer, artist and librettist, perform. A notice pinned to the side of the Arts Club entrance advertising an art exhibition drew my attention so in I popped to take a look and promptly enjoyed the chatter of the gentleman on duty, the very same Bob Devereaux, describing to me each of the paintings and the artist. In the background, I could hear beautiful piano music playing but it was not coming from the exhibition room we were in, so I asked Bob where the music was being played. When he told me someone was practicing the piano up in the theatre, I was delighted, suddenly remembering this little theatre and realising it was only a short walk from the flat. Bob invited me to go take a look, so I did, and what a nice surprise. A melodious classical piece of music was being lovingly played on an upright piano by a lady who was totally oblivious of my presence until she stopped and I made myself heard. Two hours later, Christine Penberthy and I, having exhausted ourselves talking, were joined by Bob, who had closed the gallery at 5.30 p.m. He gave us an impromptu rendition of a poem he'd written about the sea. It was magical re-discovering this little gem of a theatre, meeting Christine, who was also an artist, and getting to know more of the very talented, Bob Devereaux, who had not recognised me.

Back at the flat, feeling pretty elated but utterly dumbfounded to realise that the Arts Club had been on the doorstep of the Sugar "n" Spice coffee bar in St Andrew's Street that I had managed in the '60s and I had hardly noticed its exterior. It is a significant building at the end of

Lambeth Walk and the start of The Warren. The exterior is unique in St Ives as the only remaining building with shiplap boarding to the upper storey where, according to Bob, during severe weather the building shakes from the battering of the waves, which often go over the roof. Pouring myself a glass of refreshing Co-op Pinot Grigio, I sat gazing out of the red bedroom's huge sash window down Lifeboat Hill towards the harbour. I watched the holiday makers in their various modes of casual wear, shorts, t-shirts, sandals and white legs, vowing I would discover every nook and cranny of this town that I had spectacularly neglected all those years ago. As I look out thinking this, there before me, is a rectangular granite building, The Market House, built in 1832, replacing a much earlier building. Until the present Guildhall was built, The Market House's upper floor was occupied by the Town Hall, where the Mayor was also the Chief Magistrate. It provided two cells for prisoner's and many a hardened smuggler was brought to trial in the courtroom. The Market Place itself was at the heart of the medieval town. St Ives Borough Charter of 1639 enabled the town to hold a market there twice a week. All this history on my doorstep and in front of me, heavens I'd got a lot to learn.

With leisurely determination, I would set out each day after studying my personal bible, the tide table. This would decide a particular direction for that day and I would simply, go with the flow, spending as much time walking on the beach and through the water wherever possible but always ending with an area of the town to explore. The magical names of Salubrious Place, Court Cocking, Virgin Street, Teetotal Street, Pudding Bag Lane, Fish Street, Barnoon Hill, The Digey and the steep flight of Academy Steps – where I first lived right at the top in a bedsit, now smartly named, Academy Flat. It brought back many memories, one being that I could once fly up those steps two at a time. Seeing them now gave me the jitters just looking up at them – could I really have been that other person? Another challenge – to get up Academy

Steps, maybe not two at a time, but a jaunty skip up, and out onto Barnoon Hill, once I'd practiced.

Delicatessen's, fresh vegetables, cheese shops, bakeries, surf shops Mountain Warehouse, plenty of card shops, gift shops, jewellers and art galleries fill the main shopping drag of Fore Street, each with their goods beautifully displayed onto the pavement vying for attention as people swarmed up and down the narrow cobbled street creating a buzzy holiday atmosphere. It didn't take me long to recapture what I always called "the back streets of Naples", meaning I got to know every back street, alleyway, steps, and shortcuts to avoid the madding crowd and realised very quickly how adept I was at this. It was interesting to see how far I could get from say, The Market Place to Porthmeor Beach during the day without seeing anyone, or hardly anyone within a distance of approximately five hundred yards. This also avoided the temptation of being bedazzled by the many food shops selling aroma tempting pies, pasties, croissants, scone's and a variety of freshly made coffees.

At the end of Fore Street down onto Wharf Road opposite the slipway were a couple of shops up the top of some steps, there I discovered, to my sheer delight, the Moomaid of Zennor Ice Cream Parlour – I'm very fond of ice cream of course and usually walk faster with my eyes averted past the many shops and outlets selling the tempting product, especially being in St Ives in one of the hottest summers on record – but it wasn't the ice cream that attracted my attention, it was the fact that this ice cream was made in Zennor, a small village out on the coast road towards Lands' End where I once lived. Wild horses wouldn't have stopped me climbing the few steps where, at the entrance to Moomaid was a massive picture covering one wall showing cows grazing in the fields of Zennor surrounding my enchanting, end-of-row granite cottage with the words "The Factory" written above it. Indeed, the cows grazing in the fields were The Factory of Moomaid where the ice cream was produced on the nearby farm, Tremedda. With a scrumptiously tempting variety of flavours to choose from, I eventually came out of my comfort zone of vanilla and plumped for a Shipwreck sugar cone filled with sea salt, caramel and honeycomb ice cream topped with clotted cream – to say it was delicious would be an understatement. Sitting on the slipway wall relishing this delight whilst watching the colourful fishing boats bobbing away in the harbour, felt like heaven.

A few yards further along from Moomaid is the iconic Sloop Inn, where I tasted my very first beer, and where, as a group of friends in the sixties, we met regularly making it our own special place – outside in the summer, inside during the cold winter months. The sign on the Sloop Inn shows a date earlier than the Parish Church 1434, although its origins cannot be proved. Its central location has ensured its importance as a meeting place, used by generations of the fishing community as well as artists, who began to visit the town in the 1880s. Drawings of fishermen still cover the walls. The outside area on the wharf now has tables and benches where people can eat and drink in a civilised manner in the area cordoned off by a rope chain – whereas we used to stand outside in various groups, clutching our drinks while putting the world to rights.

Discovering St Ives anew was captivating. I loved walking along the harbour; round onto Wharf Road and onto Smeaton's Pier watching the fishermen haul in their catches of pilchards and mackerel from their traditional Cornish fishing boats. It is hard to believe that St Ives was once a bustling port containing hundreds of fishing boats. Before the railway was built, all goods came in and out of town by sea, and the job of The Customs Officer was one of the most important in the town. Behind Porthmeor Road, I discovered a straight lane called The Ropewalk. This is where rope was made for the fishing industry, and it was adjacent to the great cellars and lofts for processing the millions of pilchards brought ashore every autumn during the 19th century for export to Italy. Fish cellars and sail lofts abound that lower central part of St Ives. The first building of the wooden Porthmeor Studios complex was constructed in the mid-1800s for the pilchard fishing industry. When fishing declined at the end of that century, the artists began to move in. Now the last original building along Porthmeor Beach, it recently received major funding to preserve it for both artists and fishermen.

My heart went out to these beloved people of St Ives, the fishermen, their wives, their children, and their families, seeing for the first time what a massively important role the fishing industry played in the survival of this mediaeval town. From Smeaton's Pier, my feet were always drawn towards Bamaluz Beach, a recent and new find. Bamaluz is an elusive little cove that is not there as often as it is there! Known locally as the 'secret beach' Bamaluz is only a beach at low tide. It's a great getaway spot, rarely getting busy even in the height of summer. While at midday the beach is a sun trap, it does tend to fall into the shade later in the day due to the terrace of tall houses behind. Bamaluz is located between the harbour and Porthgwidden Beach and is accessed by a set of steep steps just in front of the St Ives Museum at Wheal Dream. A testament once again to the fishermen, this museum was once a pilchard cellar, and the first floor had been the home of the Seaman's Mission.

I believe that my real attraction to Bamaluz was that local author Phil Moran's (a friend of many moons ago) series of Soggy Bear books begins. Soggy is left on top of a sandcastle as the tide comes in getting washed out to sea only to be rescued by a local fisherman.

Every bend and turn, every nook and cranny revealed a past fish cellar, a sail loft and, a testament to the future, art gallery upon art gallery. These two major important industries to St Ives seemed to marry together, albeit one in the decline and the other with a glittering future. After all, a plaque commemorating the home of the artist and mariner Alfred Wallis is placed on one of the cottages in Back Road West. A self-taught painter, Wallis was "discovered" by the artists Ben Nicholson and Christopher Wood in 1928. His naïve images of the sea and the town inspired a new generation of young modernist painters.

Porthgwidden Beach, the smallest of St Ives's four fine beaches, was once the rubbish dump for the town. Above the beach itself, animals and chickens were kept, and at the end of the nineteenth century, it became the centre for local industries including a kipper house and a box factory. Today there is no sign of its past history. A beach of soft golden sand has a piazza of beach huts and the trendy Porthgwidden Beach Café that adorns the entrance at the slipway, a charming restaurant open in the evenings, with views across the glistening water to Godrevy Lighthouse.

Directly behind Porthgwidden Beach Café is a tall building called "The Tower", where the painter, writer, and sculptor, Sven Berlin, lived and worked. Now best known for his controversial, fictionalised autobiography "The Dark Monarch" published in 1962. The book was withdrawn from sale within a few weeks of publication in Autumn 1962, due to libel actions. I remembered so clearly the furore of St Ives at the time, more particularly the artists who were up in arms about the book that dominated the headlines and the town for a long time. "The Tower" was tucked in between the Beach Café and the public toilets, and I saw the door was slightly ajar, I pushed it open gently, and with no one taking a scrap of notice, I let myself in and explored the small, tall building. Directly as I entered, a flight of scuffed stairs to the right took me to the first floor and this was where Sven Berlin lived, slept, wrote, and painted all those years ago. In the downstairs room, he created his sculptures – the interior of the building looked as it might have done during his time there – it felt eerie but full of presence, his presence I believe. The Tower nowadays seems to be used as a storeroom, and a lick of white paint on the outside blends it in with the rest of the surrounding buildings.

Leaving Porthgwidden Beach and onto the Island, I loved walking up and around to one of the most popular spots in St Ives, St Nicholas Chapel, which is dedicated to the patron saint of sailors. Well, being a sailor, I always like to pay my respects to this lovely little Chapel, looking out across the vast expanse of the Atlantic Ocean. Having sailed across this ocean twice now, I know the beauty and the perils it offers. But it's this very ocean that has captured my heart, and I feel safe and at home being surrounded by it in St Ives. Walking down from The Island, Porthmeor Beach is spread out before me with its glorious stretch of light golden sand where huge waves are pounding at its edge and surfers are out there in large numbers waiting for a "big wave" to ride, is a sight I will never tire of.

Much as I'm getting to know and enjoy all the beaches, nothing will ever touch or compare with Porthmeor in my eyes. This beach is so evocative of the past. Jess Val Baker and The Mask Pottery, Barnaloft, Piazza Studios, Porthmeor Studios (originally built in the early 1800s for the pilchard fishery), its cellars still clearly show how this industry worked, and the building was listed Grade II in 2005 because of this evidence. Fishermen still use the cellars for storing and repairing their gear and setting nets. However, Porthmeor is best known for the incredible number of internationally important artists who have worked here, including Francis Hodgkin's, Ben Nicholson, Patrick Heron, Francis Bacon and Wilhelmina Barnes-Graham. It is perhaps the oldest working artists' studio in the country, as well as having the most illustrious occupants.

All these buildings and studios with huge windows that face onto Porthmeor, where potters from the Mask used to empty out onto the beach during their break times, and artists would appear from their respective studios down a ladder from the studio window for a quick dip into the sea. It was fun, it was laid back, it was trendy, even to this day the smell of Ambre Solaire suntan oil takes me straight back to Porthmeor Beach and those sun-kissed, halcyon days.

Today it remains pretty much the same, though The Mask Pottery is no longer there. Along with the Beach Café, St Ives Surf School now takes up a good area on the beach promoting this very popular sport. Just behind the various surf stores with their brightly coloured wet suits and surfing gear, paddle boats and canoes strewn neatly across the beach making a colourful display, stands the mighty Tate St Ives Museum. It's a monument to represent the work of the iconic 20th-century artists associated with St Ives. More than anything, I was dying to see inside the Tate but resisted the urge to do so until my friend, Susan, arrived for a short visit, as I'd promised her that we would make a special day to experience this gallery together.

Coming off the beach at Porthmeor, I doubled-back onto Porthmeor Road. I loved this area of the town with its famous Porthmeor Studios and St Ives School of Painting, it was full of character and time stood still as if the very same artists of years long gone, were still present and working there. Nothing seemed to have changed. Further along Back Road West brought me to the well-known Penwith Gallery, home of the Penwith Society of Arts which moved to its present location in 1961. The Penwith Society was founded in 1949 by a group of artists in St Ives under the distinguished leadership of Ben Nicholson, Barbara Hepworth, and Bernard Leach.

For the first ten years, work was displayed in rented premises in Fore Street, mainly above The Castle Inn, and its seasonal exhibitions became a national showplace for contemporary painting, sculpture, and crafts. In 1960, the present site, then a pilchard packing factory, was acquired and converted into a gallery, with artists' studios above. In 1970, an adjacent property became available, and the artist-members, assisted by Barbara Hepworth, sought funds to create the present group of galleries, studios, and workshops. Remembering all the to-do's that went on with St Ives's notoriously volatile artistic community when The

Penwith Gallery first moved to its present site makes me smile. Only too well did I know the gallery's formidable curator, Kathleen Watkins, who ruled the gallery and its artists with a rod of iron. With such luminaries as Barbara Hepworth, Janet Leach, Bernard Leach, Ben Nicholson, and Patrick Heron – just to mention a few – to answer to, Kathleen had her work cut out.

Back Road West was certainly home to an impressive representation of artists I was beginning to discover, coming upon a plaque on the wall of one of the old cottages commemorating the home of the artist, Alfred Wallis. A self-taught painter, Wallis was "discovered" by the artists Ben Nicholson and Christopher Wood in 1928. Born in 1855, Wallis went to sea as a cabin boy at the age of nine, and from about 1880 worked as a fisherman in Cornwall. In 1890 he opened a rag-and-bone store in St Ives. After retiring from this, he did odd jobs, including selling ice cream. He began to paint in 1925 to ease the loneliness he felt after his wife's death. His naïve images of the sea and the town inspired a new generation of young modernist painters. He died in 1942.

During the 1960s, the names of artists like Alfred Wallis and Bryan Pearce were always being mentioned, more particularly Bryan Pearce who was being recognised as one of the country's foremost "naïve" painters. He was a sufferer of the condition, phenylketonuria (also called PKU), which affects the normal development of the brain. Encouraged by his mother, who was herself a painter, and by other St Ives artists, he began painting in 1953. He attended the St Ives School of Painting from 1953-1957. Of course, the café and pub life, beer and cigarette-fuelled conversations were as they were in the 60s and 70s, basically in one ear and out the other. All I really remember of that time was my love and admiration for both of these naïve painters, Alfred Wallis and Bryan Pearce (who I had briefly known).

Two steps off Back Road West takes you into Norway Square and to the entrance of the former

Mariners' Church, the home of St Ives Society of Artists. It was in the winter of 1949 that a gale-force wind hit the backwaters of this unconsecrated Mariners' Church when a Most Extraordinary General Meeting had been convened by some dissident members. A Naval Commander – a painter of sail and sea – held his fist aloft and brandished it uncomfortably close to the chin of the Chairman, a respectable, respected portraitist. The old sea-dog's quarter-deck expletives thundered and gusted within quiet walls which here-to-fore had echoed approbation or mild criticism. They now shuddered at the stormy sounds of character assassination. Brother Brushes bristled, and the Chairman resigned. The raised fist became a signal for mutiny. A number of youngish artists abandoned ship, stripping their work from the corner of the Gallery which had harboured it grudgingly for a while as a hand-across-the-sea gesture to Contemporary Art. Later, they assembled at the Castle Inn, and with the stunned Chairman placed at the helm, the new Penwith Society was christened with alcoholic bonhomie. Filled with good cheer and optimism, they returned to their studios. And thus was the split between the doyenne of traditional art, St Ives Society of Artists, and the contemporary art of The Penwith Society of Art.

To me, this seems like a natural split as I see both galleries now blossoming with an abundance of art and looking healthily successful. Plenty of room in St Ives for both traditional and contemporary art, though I expect back in those good old days every artist was living hand to mouth. "A storm in a Paint Pot" headed one journalist at the time, having written an amusing article on the whole sorry debacle.

This former Mariners' Church is an imposing building in the heart of Downalong, a prestigious location a stone's throw from the picturesque harbour has a permanent display of fine paintings and ceramics by its members – a massive building, so many artists can exhibit their work throughout the year. My eye is drawn to an exhibition in the Crypt Gallery underneath the Church, this had been used from 1946 – 1948 by the so-called, Crypt Group, a group of Modernist painters, whose initial exhibition raised not only eyebrows but brickbats from traditional artists spurred on by Harry Rowntree, the painter, illustrator, and caricaturist, who called on the frankly Modernist group to drop the "French rot" and get back to sweet sanity. Today, this exhibition by Paul Wadsworth in the Crypt Gallery would certainly have the traditionalists turning in their graves – it's modern, colourful, big and bold – my sort of painting for sure. Paul brought the gallery alive as he painted in-situ with canvases on the floor or on easels using tin foil plates for his paint: messy, exuberant but totally captivating. It delighted me to see a gallery being used, not only for exhibiting work but seeing the artist actually plying his art there for everyone to see, was inspiring.

Chapter Two

As Dark As Light

Past haunts like The Sloop Inn, The Castle, and The Life Boat Inn have all changed their image to cater for the influx of tourists. These places are no longer the hang-outs of artists, potters, poets, and misfits. When "The Life Boat Inn" first opened its doors on Wharf Road overlooking the harbour, we, as a group, all used to pile in there every night, usually after supper – standing room only, and you had to squeeze yourself in at that. It was bigger than The Sloop, and it was good for us to have a change, so we bombarded it for a good season, where it became the 'In' place to be until eventually trying to squeeze in there and get served became a mission.

Now it lives another life, with square wooden tables and chairs upholstered in boredom, where the tourists gravitate to a window seat to eat toasties and chips, knock back a pint and watch rugby. The back room of The Castle Inn in Fore Street was a favourite – backroom only because the locals inhabited it, and we could roll down Ayr Lane after dinner from Trewyn, where I was living at the time, straight to The Castle's rear entrance. A cramped snug bar where we went for a nightcap – the friendly landlords, Stan and Stella Jackson enjoyed our exuberant company and camaraderie, and this is where I met their daughter, Carol, who became one of my closest friends and still is to this day.

Visiting The Castle now was quite a shock – I popped my head through the front door as I was passing one afternoon to take a peep. The whole place had been knocked through from front to back so no cosy snug there anymore. Music trickled out from a tired trio, and the TV was showing football, rugby or cricket while people ate large plates of food in front of it.

Gone to another planet have *The Lifeboat* and *The Castle,* but *The Sloop Inn* remains spiritually the home of the '60s and the '70s. Not too much devastating change here apart from the cordoned off front and much larger eating space inside. Now an Inn where you can actually stay and where two glasses of wine cost more than a weeks' pay way back then.

Explore, explore, explore, I couldn't get enough of it. Every nook and cranny seemed to hold another story I knew nothing about. The attraction I felt towards and being drawn to walk to and around Pedn Olva rocks and point when the tide was out was like a drug drawing me towards it. Something of a strangely mysterious nature lurked there, and I couldn't quite get it into my head that someone would build a hotel perched high atop of those rocks. Apart from the stunning view, it appeared to be in a hugely precarious and dangerous position.

Curiosity soon killed the cat – and it came to me without even a search. A mine, some sort of tin or copper mine and I was right. I had always been attracted to the tin mining industry of Cornwall, especially around the St Just and Pendeen area. Botallack Mine, The Count House, the iconic Crowns Engine Houses, Levant Mine and Geevor, all mines that I have explored and been utterly fascinated with. It's the industrial part of Cornish heritage that interests me – perhaps it stems from my own background of the cotton mill industry that I was privileged to be born into.

And on top of Pedn Olva rocks there once stood an engine house, Pedn Olva Engine House, Pedn Olva Mine (North Wheal Providence). An old copper mine, which was first worked in the 18th century, when an adit was driven westwards under St Ives town from Pedn Olva Point, reminding us that the area was originally an important one for mining tin. The mine at this location was never explored as it was believed to be unsafe, and the building became an artist's studio. The engine house was demolished in the early 20th century. Its staircase was incorporated in the Pedn Olva Hotel, which now occupies its site.

My feet are happiest bare-footed pounding water and scrunching sand, and I intended to do as much of this as I possibly could on this special journey. Feeling the earth beneath your feet without a piece of leather or rubber in between feels natural, and in my case, touches the elements of the ocean in the water and the magnetic elements of the earth on the sand. Pedn Olva Mine that was, or never was, must have had the promise of mineral surrounding it so near the sea, and at most times, way below it. Some magnetic pull attracted me to this area, like the Crowns Engine Houses at Botallack Mine, that perch perilously on the rocks above the raging sea – these also drew me towards them. I find myself oddly attracted to the Pedn Olva Hotel, where I often pop in to read the daily newspapers with a coffee after a walk or enjoy a sundowner on the top terrace with its stunning views. I'm happy pottering about the charming hotel, and the staff seems unfazed by my presence as if being there is perfectly natural.

Pedn Olva steps lead up from just outside the hotel to the railway station. Taking a right turn at the top takes you up Station Hill above to The Malakoff. In the 1970s, the Round Table created the Malakoff Gardens on the seaward side, named after the 1855 Crimean battle. On the other side of the road, the buildings on The Terrace, overlooking the harbour, were the first homes built for the town's gentry, high above the fishing smells. Originally a private road, it soon became the main entrance to the town. At the back of The Terrace, the houses are the more illustrious homes of the said gentry. Most remarkably, of course, would be Talland House, the home that Virginia Woolf spent three months every year on holiday with her family, and was the inspiration for her novel "To the Lighthouse". This rather grand house has some of the most stunning views, especially from the balcony across to Godrevy Lighthouse, a view that inspired Virginia Woolf to write her most famous novel, where she was at her happiest in a home that she loved. I too lived there briefly in the 1960s at the top of the house under the eaves in a flat with dormer windows. It was really very nice with lovely views that I remembered, and no Virginia Woolf. Alas today, she would have been as shocked as I was to see blocks of "luxury" apartments replacing those elegant houses and blocking what were truly "magnificent" views. Shame upon the councillors and town planners of Penwith Borough Council!

Wimbledon and the World Cup frenzy were being televised during the beginning of my stay at the Quirky flat. Being a mad tennis fan, a follower of the ATP Tour and the Grand Slams, I was looking forward to a fortnight of unadulterated viewing on the little TV. The landlady had described the TV and a black box as being fairly new, but I remember having such a TV myself thirty light years ago, so I guessed it must have been new to her. My first attempt at switching on failed miserably – I followed the sheet of instructions from the landlady's info folder, but no matter how I tried tuning the damn thing, nothing happened, just fuzz on the screen. In sheer desperation, I went to the craft shop beneath the flat and asked the shop assistant if she had any idea how to work a television. Jo assured me that she was very savvy where TV's were concerned and in her lunch break came up to give the TV the benefit of her knowledge. She baulked when she saw the TV, the black box and the miles of iffy looking wiring. But savvy Jo could not tune that TV any more than I could. Seeing my huge disappointment at having to miss Wimbledon and the World Cup, Jo suddenly burst forth that she could lend me a TV and would bring it round the following day.

As good as her word, Jo arrived at the flat the next morning, heaving the largest box imaginable up the flight of stairs into the flat. Together we dismantled the small TV, the black box, a mass of wiring and the aerial plus two remotes. "Health and Safety would have a field day with all this," Jo spluttered exhaustively pointing at the heap we'd piled up on the floor as she struggled to get the new TV out of its polystyrene casing. And indeed it was a brand new out-of-the-box TV – Wow! I was suitably impressed at the flat screen state-of-the-art model now sitting perfectly, filling the space left by its smaller counterpart on the large ledge of the sash window as if it were made for it. Aerial and plug socket sorted, one press of the remote and hey presto! One beautiful picture and all channels imaginable. Wimbledon came on like a magic light and I honestly could have been in the front seat of centre court – heaven!

Jo explained to me that I was very lucky as she was about to sell the TV as she'd bought it just as her boyfriend and his TV moved in with her, so she'd been storing it in her garage. I asked how much she wanted for it and the £100 she mentioned from the original price of £200 made me jump in feet first, and I offered to buy it. Jo was thrilled, I was delighted, but as yet had not consulted the landlady. We managed to store the old TV plus all its bits and pieces in the red bedroom wardrobe until I decided how to approach the landlady. If push came to shove, I might well have to put the old TV back. In the meantime, I was going to enjoy a few days of unadulterated Wimbledon and World Cup viewing. In a burst of patriotism and entering into the spirit of the World Cup I bought a large England flag which by some dangerous effort, I managed to attach to a flagpole on the wall outside one of the sash windows. One of the benefits of living alone bang in the Market Place of St Ives, is you always have company from The Golden Lion pub, if you happen to have the windows wide open like I did being such a hot summer. Every time I heard a massive cheering, I knew that England had scored a goal. It was so loud and infectious that I might as well have been in the Golden Lion myself.

After a brilliant weekend of sport, my conscience got the better of me and I decided it was time to send an email to my dear landlady regarding the new television. Wording this as best I could, throwing slight emphasis on the wiring being very dodgy with too much of it, and a loose aerial connection before adding a bonus on the end suggesting that we shared the cost of the beautiful new television . . . I pressed the send button. A couple of hours later, my iPhone pinged and a reply came through from the landlady expressing her sheer delight at my taking the initiative of installing a new television. She thanked me for doing this and for sharing the cost. Yay! So no recriminations. Jo, Sarah, and Maxine from the craft shop below had led me to think the landlady was some sort of professor who read a lot and never looked at the television – so it was a nice surprise to receive such a positive response.

Shopping was a great novelty. Being in the Market Place enabled me to walk to all the convenience shops, literally a stone's throw away. Shopping itself is not high on my list – but one does need to eat, and so I made shopping as pleasant as I could. Harvey Brothers Traditional Butchers in Tregenna Place was a firm favourite, so friendly and full of old charm from the nice butchers serving there that I found myself eating a lot more meat than I normally would. Much to my shock, but a pleasant surprise, the hardware store, Colenso's, in Gabriel Street, was still there, up and running just as I had left it.

St Ives library across the road from Colenso's was a great asset and the staff unbelievably friendly and helpful when I had tentatively asked if they had a copy of the controversial book by Sven Berlin, "The Dark Monarch". A senior librarian on duty produced a smile and informed me that they had got a copy of the book which she would bring down from somewhere upstairs whilst I filled in a form to become a member of the library. With membership card tucked in my wallet and "The Dark Monarch" safely in my bag, I walked up the Stennack in search of the laundry and the medical centre.

In Street-an-Pol I find myself at the Visitor Information Centre located in The Guildhall, the home of the St Ives Town Council since it was built in 1939. Outside is Barbara Hepworth's sculpture "Dual Form", which she presented to the town in 1968 to commemorate receiving the Freedom of the Borough of St Ives that year, along with artist Ben Nicholson and potter Bernard Leach. You can also get married and have your reception at this impressive building, and a weekly Farmers Market is held in the side hall every Thursday and never a sight has been more welcome – choc-full of local seasonal food and drink, Cornish produce, vegetables, fruit, fish, meat, cheese, bread, cakes, and handmade chocolate. But for me it has to be Ruby June's Indian Kitchen stall that wins the day with her rich, creamy Korma, Madras and Tikka Masala sauces all made with a variety of fresh spices, garlic, ginger and coconut deliciously permeating the market, along with freshly made Nan bread it's hard to drag myself away from Ruby's stall – when I do manage to do so, I've enough food packed neatly into a small brown carrier bag to last me for three days, and I'm in heaven. The Saffron Arts and Crafts Market is open in the same hall on Tuesdays and lots of other days, especially during the holiday season and Christmas. This is a vibrant market full of locally crafted products, affordable art, ceramics, wool crafts, wood crafts, John Chard's wonderful photography, and much more. Discovering the Guildhall and all it offers has been a great good find.

One of the most charming traditions that touched my heartstrings were the St Ives Fisherman's Lodges and their history dating back to 1900. Three lodges were opened in October 1901 – the Shamrock and Shore Shelter on the 12th and the Rose on the 19th. The lodges are meeting places. Members pay a small annual fee. Practically all fishermen belonged to lodges, which were all-male preserves. Here they did a lot of waiting about – which went with the job – keeping an eye on the boat, mustering before going to sea, waiting for the tide or for the weather to improve.

Notices to mariners were sent to the lodges from the Customs House. Some men spent nearly all day at the lodge, and wives sometimes complained that their husbands spent more time at the lodge than at home. Flags were flown when local people marry – traditionally paid for with a bag of coal – and at half-mast when they die. When Wharf Road was built, the Rose and Shore Shelters were re-sited to their present position opposite Fore Street Methodist Church, where the flag tradition still carries on. Flags are flown when a local marries – and at half-mast when they die. Sitting by these lodges, looking out across the harbour, watching the fishing boats coming in with the tide, gives me a feeling of déjà vu.

I'm mesmerised by every nook and cranny of this town, the history of the once-thriving fishing industry weaves itself into the very fabric of St Ives, it was St Ives and still is St Ives, no matter which way you look at it. Now the colossus of the art industry has eclipsed the fishing with its mass of galleries in every shape and form using the old sail lofts, cellars and packing sheds once used by the weather-worn and gnarled-handed fishermen. But that's progress, and now the town thrives as one of the UK's most popular tourist destinations pumping millions of pounds into the Cornish economy every year. When I last lived in St Ives in the early seventies there was a handful of galleries, The Penwith Gallery, the St Ives Society of Artists in the Old Mariners Chapel, the New Craftsman in Fore Street, and the Marjorie Parr Gallery in Wills Lane were the prominent galleries in those days.

Today the galleries in St Ives are in breath-taking abundance. The New Craftsman is still very much in business, and better than ever, showing some superb art, pottery and jewellery exhibitions. It remains a great favourite amongst art, pottery and jeweller collectors as well as tourists to the town who are not intimidated by entering this Fore Street shop as they might be by a larger art gallery. Unfortunately, the Marjorie Parr – Wills Lane

Gallery no longer exists. The Penwith Gallery and The St Ives Society of Artists in the Old Mariners Chapel and The Crypt Gallery are a testament to the early schools of artists in St Ives that the forefathers of these particular galleries would be proud of.

The newer generation of galleries like The Porthminster Gallery, Belgrave Gallery, Imagination Gallery, Art Space Gallery, Alexandra Dickens Studio Gallery, Millennium Gallery, St Ives Ceramics, The Barbara Hepworth Museum and, of course, the mighty Tate St Ives Museum, are but a mere fraction of what is on offer to see and discover in this unique and exquisite art colony. If I wrote in praise for the rest of my life how much this mediaeval town has blossomed on the wings of fishing, art, pottery, jewellery, sculpture, and surfing, I could never do it justice.

It's good to see most of the shops busy, bustling and full of people. It would have taken a courageous person to open a delicatessen in the middle of Fore Street, in what was once, The Craftsman, a small but very popular shop in the sixties selling pottery and crafts of every description and a place where I once started a love affair. The New Craftsman, two shops further along, followed The Craftsman which eventually closed as the newer and much larger premises took over.

Today, the New Craftsman is one of the town's finest galleries, offering a delightful mix of paintings, pots, jewellery, and glass by famous artists and affordable newcomers. It is the oldest established Art Gallery and Craft shop in St Ives. I feel totally at home in the New Craftsman, I think I must have spent a great deal of time in that shop one way or another. For old times' sake, I do some shopping in the Allotment Deli, that was once the old Craftsman, hoping that some recognition of a past affair might jump out at me, but it was not meant to be. I buy the delicious-looking fresh fruit and vegetables, bread and cheeses, chat to the busy staff, knowing I'm doing it for the wrong reasons (prices are way above my budget) but feel compelled to support this charming shop in fond memory of the past.

Opposite the delicatessen is Mountain Warehouse, a vast sprawling emporium dedicated to the pursuit of the great outdoors from camping, hiking, running, walking, swimming, fishing, canoeing, and surfing. I'm an outdoor person who loves sailing, tennis, swimming, and walking, so it's very difficult for me to by-pass the tempting "reduced" offers that spill out onto the pavement. It used to be Woolworth's in days gone by, now this swanky store has its right of place in a town that encourages an outdoor lifestyle with all the many sea and shore-based activities it has to offer. You could once enter Woolworths from Wharf Road as well as from Fore Street. The entire Woolworths building was three floors of prime property, but the ground floor wharf-side has been blocked off from the other two floors and is now home to Pizza Express.

Chapter Three

Call Of The Waves

Fancying a longer walk bright and early one morning, I decided to take myself off up Barnoon Hill to Barnoon Church and Cemetery. There seriously could not be a more stunning location for your final resting place. Perched on the hill above Porthmeor Beach, this cemetery looks out over the beautiful white sands and turquoise seas, out to Man's Head and beyond. I don't think it is possible to find a better cemetery view. For years, I harboured a strong desire to be buried in Barnoon Cemetery as I whizzed up and down Porthmeor Hill with a surfboard trying to be "with it" by learning to surf. But my efforts at surfing failed miserably and soon realised that I might end up in Barnoon Cemetery sooner than I thought – so surfing had to stop. I was in my early twenties at the time. However, I would have been in good company, as I shifted through the terraces of the graveyard and came upon the tiled tomb of artist and mariner, Alfred Wallis. His tomb is covered by an elaborate gravestone made from tiles by Bernard Leach, depicting a tiny mariner at the foot of a huge lighthouse and the words inscribed: 'Into Thy Hands O Lord.' On the outer granite wall of the church is a sign saying 'Holy Water Overflow' with a pipe sticking out from the cement joining two granite slabs. Nothing was flowing out of the seemingly dry pipe, so no Holy Water to quench my gathering thirst.

From Barnoon Cemetery, I can see part of the roof structure of the newly renovated Tate St Ives Museum – it's like a grassed out area with oblong opaque glass structures placed neatly and evenly into it. Not being able to resist the temptation, I make my way over to the rear end of the building and surprisingly discover that there are some really nice sitting areas built into this particular roof design. It's quiet and peaceful with not a soul about so I sit and make myself at home. There is a glass door entrance to the Tate building across from where I am sitting and realise it must be the staff entrance as it is adjacent to the reserved parking area of the car park. A couple of men are talking by the doorway but seem oblivious to me, so I carry on sitting and enjoying the view over the rooftop lawn and out to sea. I'm tempted to stay as it must be the only place in St Ives where there are no people, but instead, make a mental note to visit this place more often. Having no outside area at the flat, this is the perfect place to bring a book or a newspaper to read in the fresh air with a view, away from the crowds.

Luckily, I find that there's a flight of steps leading down to Porthmeor Road, which I take, then make a left turn as I've decided to take a walk along the coastal path towards Man's Head and through the kissing gate to Clodgy Point. But as I'm about to cross over to Beach Road – the start of the coastal path, I spot what looks like an ancient granite water well set back in the wall. It looks disused and a bit overgrown, but my curiosity is greater than my flip-flops and I brave the grassy walk up to it. There is a granite plaque with the inscription:

VENTON IA

The Holy Well of St Ia

Until 1843 the main water supply for Downalong

This was a pretty amazing discovery. Not in the sense that its appeared out of nowhere – it is just the mere disbelief that this once attractive looking well could have possibly been the main water source for the whole of Downalong, the area between The Wharf and Porthmeor Beach – Fish Street, Back Road West, Norway Square, and the list goes on. I suppose before 1843, the volume of local inhabitants would have been a great deal less than it is today, but, even then it's mind-boggling to think villagers had to get their water from this well for their everyday needs and most probably for the fishing industry.

With my mind whirling about the arduous tasks of the fishwives and the bal maidens in those bygone days, I made my way to Beach Road and the coastal path. This is a walk for the stout-hearted and stout-booted only if you are planning to go all the way to Zennor, but I'm not going that far as I only have my favourite flip-flops on and seriously would not feel confident doing the longer six-mile walk by myself. Today, I just want to have a complete change from the narrow cobbled streets, the charming shops and the picturesque harbour of St Ives and head out as far as Clodgy Point which is about as far as my inappropriate footwear will take me. This part of the famous South West Coastal path is truly beautiful, with amazing sea views the entire way. As I near Man's Head, I look back to see Porthmeor Beach glimmering in the distance. Further round and through the kissing gate where I spot the ruins of the Klavji (literally "sick house"), the old leper hospital, whose name has gradually become 'Clodgy Point'. Gazing out across the amazing Atlantic Ocean, I feel exhilarated, then my heart stops as my attuned eye sees in the distance, a pod of dolphins – *how lucky is that?* I tell myself.

I am relieved that I chose not to wear sensible walking shoes today as the temptation to walk the path to Zennor, would have been irresistible. I felt it wasn't safe for me to do this walk alone, it's a rugged walk, one needs to watch one's step every inch of the way, as well as taking in the spectacular views. This one is not for the faint-hearted. I'll wait until Susan arrives, then we can do the walk together. Making myself comfortable on a rocky outcrop of grass, I settle down taking in all the sights and sounds around me, the waves crashing up against the rocks below, the gulls circling above, the clear blue sky, the sun beating down, and the fresh salty air. O, how I love it!

A few yards behind The Flat is Trewyn Gardens.

This is a lovely surprise of a small St Ives garden, hidden away but bang in the middle of the town. A green and tidy lawn is ringed by sub-tropical plants and inviting benches. It's such a secret spot with a real sense of calm and a favourite lunching spot of the locals. I pass through these gardens on a very sentimental journey to see Trewyn House. Once the home of the sculptor, John Milne, who passed away in 1978, Trewyn was and still is a beautiful house. John's studio was at the bottom of the lovely garden and backed onto the studio and garden of the well-known sculptor, Barbara Hepworth.

One day – many moons ago when I was in-between jobs – John asked me if I could help out at Trewyn which he ran as an exclusive guesthouse, for friends, artists, filmmakers and in one or two cases, film stars. When John told me accommodation and food was thrown in, I was over the moon and accepted immediately. Life at Trewyn was the greatest experience imaginable. John's friend and partner at the time, Ivaldo Ferrari, an Italian of great passion, a brilliant chef with a temper to die for, cooked breakfast each morning, dinner was optional on three nights of the week – bookings only.

Practically all the illustrious guests who stayed at Trewyn booked dinner, having heard it was an experience in itself. The menu was always a "one-off" three-course meal that both John and Ivaldo planned meticulously. We all dined together at two refectory tables, where John was the perfect host. The house permeated heavenly smells when the cooking of rich garlicky, Italian and French cuisine was taking place. Guests who had not put their name down for dinner in the morning, soon changed their mind once the aroma's filled the air. St Ives restaurants lost many a booking to Ivaldo Ferrari's prima donna cuisine. My role at Trewyn was front of house and general dogsbody, but I loved it, loved the elegance, the beautiful music John played, loved the people and the outrageous Ivaldo. Trewyn was a very special house, and my time living there formed a special place in my heart.

Today, I am excitedly going to visit Trewyn again and meet the present owners, Tony and Barbara, a couple who appear to live there on their own. Trewyn is a mansion with huge rooms and a sweeping staircase. In my day it had seven bedrooms, so I'm not sure what they were doing in such a large house all by themselves. I had dropped a letter into their post box asking if I might visit the house and meet them. Tony phoned and said they would be delighted to see me. So here I am at the allotted time, at the Richmond Place entrance, pressing the doorbell on the side of the double iron-gated entrance that immediately swings open. These beautiful gates have replaced our single wooden gate next to the garage as the main entrance. The smaller entrance of double iron gates is on the other side of the property in Ayr Lane.

It all feels very familiar, but somehow it's not. I look around me to find something I might remember, but it's just not there. Rounding the end of the small driveway, there in front of me at the end of a sweeping lawn stands Trewyn. I long for some joy to spring into my heart, some recognition of those heady days and beautiful nights, but no, nothing sings out to me. Knowing that Tony and Barbara can see me from the house, I make my way up a flight of granite steps and find myself at the once familiar and large front door with the same brass doorknob and knocker that opens before I can think.

Tony is very tall and his wife, Barbara, is small. They are a delightful couple and make me feel very welcome. They have a few questions to ask me about Trewyn in the earlier days when John Milne owned it, one of the questions being, had Princess Margaret stayed there? Unfortunately, I had to burst their glimmer of hope and tell them that to my knowledge she had never stayed at Trewyn, if she had, I would surely have heard about it. Disappointment prevailed in their eyes as I sat in the sumptuous lounge that once entertained well-known people such as Patricia Neal, Roald Dahl, actor Keith Barron, and film director, John Schlesinger to name but a few. Spotting a grand piano in one corner of the room and remarking on this, Tony told me they had bought it for their granddaughter who was a keen pianist. He then embarked upon telling me that their children and grandchildren came to stay quite frequently and that's why they wanted such a large house and a house which they love.

My viewing of the house was limited to the ground floor. It was enough, and I was grateful to have been afforded the privilege. Tony and Barbara were not the owners after John died, but they bought if from a gentleman who had fallen on hard times, was in great debt, and needed to realise funds urgently. So in stepped Tony at exactly the right time, and bought Trewyn. John Milne had impeccable taste and an eye for design which manifested itself in the very fabric and being that was Trewyn in the '60s and '70s. The gardens were glorious and rich in shrubs of colour surrounding the green, green grass of the lawn. His sculpture studio – now looking more like a garden shed – was where he mostly worked and was surrounded by sub-tropical trees and shrubs – all gone now and given over to car parking space. The previous Trewyn still remains as does the garden, but with someone else's taste. Trewyn is not and never will be, the beautiful house that it once was – a precious gem in the heart of St Ives.

Needing to clear my head of Trewyn and another life, I decided a brisk walk was the answer and made my way up Ayr Lane towards the top of Porthmeor Hill. Below, Porthmeor Beach looked balmy in the late afternoon at low tide, and there were not too many people, so I hurled myself down there, slipped off my Reefs and walked through the glorious water letting the waves splash against my legs – how refreshing it was. Making my way around the Island, I decided upon a quick climb up to the Coastguard Lookout Station where the St Ives Coastguard is a volunteer Cliff, Search and Water Rescue SAR Team that do a sterling job. I receive a cheery wave from a couple of men on duty – they're used to seeing me up there, and we often have a chat about boats, the weather, The National Coastwatch Institution (NCI) Eyes Along The Coast – entirely manned by volunteers. I have such admiration for these people and I'm happy in their company. On my first visit there some weeks previously, I was exploring around outside the Coastguard building and found underneath a small dug-out room where they were selling second hand books for peanuts in an effort to raise some funding – an honesty box sat next to the books, and I saw that it was empty. Rather sad in a way, but instead of buying a couple of books which I really didn't need, and something about this effort to raise funds endeared me to these valiant people, I gave them my paddle boarding costs as a donation. What the hell! Learning to paddle board could wait another year.

For the most part, I have done what I came to do in St Ives in the period of time I could spare to be away from South Africa and my work there. Having said that, it would perhaps take years to discover every nook and cranny. But I feel I've done a pretty good job. I ferreted through the delightful cobbled streets, climbed up and down most steps leading to yet another row of cottages. Also, I explored back street alleys, discovered ancient stone archways leading to quaint courtyards and ventured into the street, roads and passages such as Court Cocking, Virgin Street, Salubrious Place, The Digey, Teetotal Street, and Fish Street. It reads like a who's who of thought-provoking names open to ridicule.

Iconic Mr. Peggotty's Disco was an absolute delight for me to see again. It was magical, and a must place to dance the night away. Opening in the mid-sixties, it took St Ives bohemian, flower-power, and art community by storm, as there was nowhere else remotely like it. Just down from the Island and at the start of Porthmeor Road in a converted sail loft, someone took a chance to open Mr. Peggotty's and never looked back. I clearly remember being there on the opening night. A crowd of us left The Sloop after closing time and headed off up Fish Street towards Back Road West weaving our way to Porthmeor Road until we found the entrance to Mr. Peggotty's. We had a complete blast and danced ourselves into the ground – it was a revelation having something as trendy as this in the town, and everyone who loved discos felt elated. But it wasn't my particular scene. I went there at most a couple of times after the opening night, and that was it. The euphoria it caused, and the pleasure it gave to the St Ives adolescent community over the years, and where so many romances took place was second-to-none. Now seeing where this iconic disco once stood really touched me. In 2008, the developers moved in and gutted it.

Susan is coming down for a few days' break from working in London, and I'm looking forward to seeing her and for our planned visit to the Tate St Ives Museum. It's a pleasure for me to go and meet her from the train as the walk to the station has to be the best in Britain by far. Waiting for the little train from St Erth to St Ives chugging in is a lovely experience – sitting at the small, outside café drinking coffee and reading the paper or looking out over Porthminster Beach is something I hadn't yet done, and it couldn't be more perfect. The train arrives, and Susan hops off with her wheelie case. She knows St Ives fairly well, though I don't think she's ever arrived at the station before and she is enchanted by it. We make our way to Pedn Olva steps and The Warren, chatting away nineteen to the dozen – we take the Lambeth Walk route to go along the seafront and harbour, taking a left at the lifeboat station up Lifeboat Hill to Market Place and The Flat. Susan loved The Flat immediately, its quirkiness, its location – small as it might be, she at once, knew that I felt at home there.

Susan's trip was only for four days, so we had to plan our visit to the Tate and plumped for a couple of days into her stay. In the meantime, it was free range to do a little exploring, beach walking and generally taking in the atmosphere of St Ives. I saw that Susan was in her element just being away from work and enjoying the freedom to walk around with flip-flops on. She was fascinated by the two young men on Smeaton's Pier selling sushi and seafood from an old Citroen van and jumped for joy spotting The Oyster Cart in Fore Street just down from the New Craftsman. Strolling along the Wharf, we noticed an eye-catching board outside *The Searoom Gastrobar* advertising St Ives Gin, a really attractive poster in turquoise blue with a picture of Smeaton's Pier, the lighthouse, Kitty's Corner and some fishing boats bobbing on the water.

Neither of us liked gin, but we were fascinated to know more about Saint Ives Liquor Co (SILCo). The outside tables of *The Searoom* were all taken, looking inside, it was also full with a nice, vibey atmosphere – "pity we couldn't have lunch here," I remarked to Susan, "I quite fancy a good crab gratin." Before leaving, my eye caught a rather nice display of St Ives Gin set out on a wooden dresser – the bottles of different sizes were attractive in themselves – *the oblong-block glass bottles emblazoned with the colourful labels, would make a lovely gift for someone who liked and appreciated the different infusions used to create this unique gin*, I thought.

Doing a bit more research on SILCo back at the flat, Susan discovered the distillery was in Zennor, started by the Thompson family whom she knew quite well many years ago. We had both attended Pete and Tamsin's wedding at Zennor in the eighties, now here they were with their grown up children, having created in 2014, Saint Ives Liquor Co. We both made a mental note to have lunch at *The Searoom* during the next couple of days.

The Tate morning dawns, and we're both pretty excited. Coffee and croissants, followed by a nice brisk walk along Porthminster Beach and back, put us in a good frame of mind for the day – nothing else planned but to visit this award-winning Tate St Ives Museum. Nothing of this magnitude has happened in St Ives before, nor has anything had such an effect on its economy – visitors flocking to this prize-winning museum were beyond the Tate's wildest dreams – boosting tourism to an absolute maximum.

Inspiring art and breath-taking scenery meet at Tate St Ives. Perched above Porthmeor Beach with views across the Atlantic Ocean, the gallery showcases some of the best-loved British artworks of the 20th Century. I am about to discover how a small fishing village became art capital of the world.

Of course, I shall be seeing Tate St Ives Museum for the first time with the new 1,200 square metres extension to the existing gallery that was completed in 1993 on the site of the former gas works. The architects were commissioned to design a building for the gallery in a similar style to the gas works. The original proposal to extend produced a rash of "Stop the Tate" posters in windows throughout the town, and protests about everything from property prices being driven up by arty incomers to the loss of parking spaces. After extensive public consultation, the architects' eventual solution was to double the gallery space by excavating into the hillside behind the original building – which drove up the cost to £20m from the original estimate of £12m.

On winning the prestigious £100,000 Museum of The Year award, the most lucrative museum prize in the world, The Guardian newspaper headlined 'Breathtakingly beautiful': *Tate St Ives wins museum of the year award.* Stephen Deuchar, chair of the judging panel and director of the Art Fund, which sponsors the prize, said: "Tate St Ives tells the story of the artists who have lived and worked in Cornwall in an international context. The new extension to the gallery is deeply intelligent and breathtakingly beautiful, providing the perfect stage for a curatorial programme that is at once adventurous, inclusive, and provocative. The judges admired an architect and gallery team who devoted some 12 years to this transformational change, consulting with the local community all the way."

The imposing entrance to Tate St Ives Museum feels slightly out of context after coming along The Digey, a narrow, cobbled and ancient passageway between Fore Street and Porthmeor Road. But it's in context to everything around it, and doesn't stick out like a sore thumb, and certainly an improvement on its previous footprint, the gas works. A world-class reception greets us, and we pay our entrance fee, a concessional one for me – I presume it's my age, but don't ask. The exhibition on at present is of British artist, Patrick Heron. Behind us is a magnificent stained glass window designed by Patrick Heron, commissioned by the Tate for the new building and it's pretty spectacular, with fabulous colours and massive presence. I knew Patrick and his wife, Delia, they were a big part of my early days in St Ives. I would often visit their house, 'Eagles Nest', perched on the hill above Zennor, where the Herons were always keen to show off their lovely daughters and the garden.

Going through the first door out of the reception area, we enter a circular stairwell with windows letting in the light onto the artwork of Glasgow based artist France-Lise McGurn – Collapsing New People. What a great introduction to an artist I had never heard of. Invited through the Tate St Ives Artists' Programme, McGurn used her residency at Tate St Ives to think about the function of gossip, anecdotes, parties and the stories that circulate in an artists' colony. As she says about the stairwell: 'it is as though there could have been a party here'. I think France-Lise McGurn could be right.

Entering the galleries, I gaze about in wonderment at the familiarity of a great many of the paintings, or was it the familiar styles that I recognised so well? Roger Hilton – February 1954, stands out like an old friend. Ben Nicholson – a favourite of mine, seeing two of his pictures again makes me realise how much I love his work. John Wells, abstract artist - Untitled, Windows on the Night and Sea-Bird Forms. John was an assistant of Barbara Hepworth for eleven years. Naum Gabo called him 'the Paul Klee of the constructivist movement'. Then the incomparable Peter Lanyon – Clevedon Bandstand, painted in 1964. Thermal – painted in 1960, shortly after he began gliding. He was one of Britain's leading Modernist painters, and unlike other key figures in the St Ives School, he was born and raised in St Ives. Peter died on the 31st August 1964 as a result of injuries he received in a gliding accident – Clevedon Bandstand and Clevedon Night were painted earlier, in the year of his death.

In the middle of all these paintings is one, Pablo Picasso – Compotier, Violin, Bouteille, 1914. Set in a heavy gilt frame, this painting looks slightly out of context amongst the Cornish School, but I am a great admirer of Picasso, and the frame aside, I see the cubism, his neoclassical style and Surrealism beautifully depicted in this painting. The Cornish School is in good company, as is the great Pablo Picasso.

Bryan Wynter – Riverbed 1959 – love this picture. He lived in an isolated cottage above Zennor, near St Ives, until his death in 1975. Not in this exhibition, his painting, Gulls – 1954, is another fine example of this artist's work.

Sir Terry Frost – Roger Hilton – Denis Mitchell – Paul Feiler – Sandra Blow: just a few of St Ives artists accompanying the main exhibition, and I am singularly overwhelmed at how stunningly fantastic they all are.

Suddenly, we are in the heart of the gallery and surrounded by the distinctive artwork of Patrick Heron – there before us 'Azalea Garden' 'Five Discs', 'Four Blues with Pink', and a blaze of scarlet, pink, deep green, indigo, brilliant yellow and pale blue on larger than life canvases in this glorious gallery. I feel moved and unbelievably emotional seeing these paintings. All of them, painted by my contemporaries, my friends. In some cases, mere acquaintances, but each one of them was the hub of the St Ives art colony in the days when a painting or a drawing might be given by a struggling artist in payment for a meal. It was the same kind of feeling when visiting The Pompidou Centre in Paris and seeing the paintings of Matisse, Miro, Van Gogh, Picasso, Pissarro, and other great impressionists – such greatness, but what did they go through to get there?

Being in the Tate St Ives Museum now, seeing the works of contemporary and abstract artists who I knew long before their work reached such hallowed halls, some of their struggles, failures, successes and romantic liaisons. It leaves me with a lump in my throat that few are alive to see their work hanging in such a prestigious gallery that has just won the Museum of the Year Award 2018. I think they would be punch-drunk, overwhelmed, and very, very proud – I know that I am.

Trying to take in this permanent monument to St Ives artists past and present, as we gaze around the Rotunda of the gallery, is mind-boggling. I've just been hit by the larger-than-life painting by Sandra Blow 'Vivace', and it's certainly lively as the title suggests – wow! I love this picture. Sandra Blow moved to St Ives in the mid-1990's, way after I had left, and I know little about her, other than her cheery face and happy demeanour – she died in 2006, aged 81.

Susan suggests having lunch at the Café. This is on the top floor of the gallery with another spectacular view over St Ives, Porthmeor Beach and the ocean beyond. We find a presentable table where we can see across to the Atlantic – we are not being fobbed off by a waitress to a corner table for two where the view is a picture on the wall – no, it's the wide expanse of the blue ocean outside that is the main feature of the little Café at Tate St Ives. We both order sandwiches with a shell fish theme and a salad. It's some fancy worded menu that wouldn't go amiss in a Covent Garden eatery in London, but we're confident it will taste just as good as the menu describes. As this is such a special occasion, we each plump for a glass of wine to celebrate our venture into the world of the Tate St Ives Museum, and to the late and great artists who made it happen.

Lunch over and much revived, it wouldn't be complete to leave this splendid gallery without visiting the Tate St Ives Shop, where artists and the local landscape are its focus. We browse through the wide selection of books, gifts, postcards, and greeting cards. It also stocks jewellery as well as collectable Tate St Ives mugs. There is a wonderful collection of Tate-embossed eye-catching paraphernalia, and we were finding it hard not to purchase quite a few of the items that took our fancy, but returning to South Africa with limited baggage made this a no-go area.

However, we were in the shop and felt we did not want to end the visit without having something special to remind us, so we bought each other a print. I gave Susan Patrick Heron's, *Four Blues with Pink* and Susan gave me Sandra Blow's *Vivace*. We were both delighted with our mementos, and more so when we learned that purchasing a print, over 70% of the income is invested in the Tate St Ives Museum's education and exhibition programme. Delighted with this information, we clutched our precious prints in bright orange, TATE bags and left the portals of . . . Museum of the Year, 2018.

Tate St Ives Museum also manages the Barbara Hepworth Museum and Sculpture Garden in Barnoon Hill, and Susan suggests that we go there after alighting from the Tate, but I don't want to visit the Barbara Hepworth Museum and suggest to Susan that she visits there on her own either today, or at another time when she next pops down to Cornwall. I want to savour the lovely day we've had in the Gallery. I now feel that a pleasant walk along Porthmeor Beach, around the Island and back through Downalong to the area of converted sail lofts, pilchard cellars and packing sheds that, in some cases, became studios of the artists whose work we had just been admiring.

To be honest, I really didn't want to visit the Barbara Hepworth Museum at all. Too many memories. During my years living at Trewyn, I was privileged enough to become associated with her sculptures through the friendship between Barbara Hepworth and John Milne. One of our great friends during that time was Brian Smith, Barbara's personal assistant. Brian lived in a small cottage, a few yards away from the Hepworth studio where he worked. He was a regular visitor at Trewyn and popped in to join us for a light lunch most days. His wicked sense of humour had us in stitches until we laughed ourselves hoarse. He was protective of his boss, who he liked, respected, and devoted his time to. Dame Barbara Hepworth died in a fire at her home, Trewyn Studio on 20th May 1975. Brian Smith's hair turned white overnight from the shock.

A personal friend of mine, Norman Stocker, also worked for Barbara Hepworth in what was called at the time, The Foundry. This building was diagonally opposite Trewyn Studio on Barnoon Hill and was formerly a cinema and a Palais de Danse (dance hall). This is where Hepworth's large sculptures were created, and Norman worked on them – I often found him standing outside have a sneaky cigarette in his boiler suit literally covered in white plaster including his face and hands. I teased him mercilessly about this, warning him he might well end up a statue himself. If we met for a drink in the evening, he would look smart in a shirt and jacket, but still, his hands and face looked as if he'd contracted a rare skin condition.

I felt that having such happy memories of Trewyn, John Milne, Barbara Hepworth, Brian Smith, and Norman Stocker, should be kept safely in my memory box – these people are no longer alive, and I feel that a visit to the Barbara Hepworth Museum and Sculpture Garden would open up a gaping wound.

My time in St Ives is nearing its end. I've done what I set out to do – discover St Ives for real and get to know this beloved town with its cobbled streets, narrow passageways, higgledy-piggledy steps, the ancient archways, hidden doorways, sail lofts, cellars, the quaintest of cottages, and the streets with strange names. The hubs and the pubs, and the restaurants and shops, too many to mention but trust me they're there. Porthminster, Porthmeor, Porthgwidden, Bamaluz, and The Harbour where I feel I've trodden every grain of sand and walked endlessly through their shores. The art galleries are beyond counting, but it never ceased to amaze me the variety of paintings in the art galleries that covered the gambit for each and every tourist that visited St Ives. Something for everyone, even the hard-bitten would find it difficult not to find something to capture their fancy and take home.

Closing the door on my quirky flat is with a sad heart. But it is time to go, and I know that. Susan has booked our last two nights in St Ives at The Sloop Inn, and I couldn't have been more delighted. Strangely, after three months of the most glorious summer the UK has ever had, the weather has changed. I wake up to a drizzly day with grey skies and thick mist. Looking out of the window, I spot Annie cleaning the outside area of the Sloop in her Hi Vis jacket, getting it all ship-shape and ready for the first onslaught of customers for breakfast. Annie just does this, I don't think it's her job and the gesture and the familiarity of seeing her there at 8.30 a.m. in the morning brings a lump to my throat.

Our breakfast is served upstairs in The Captain's Table at the Sloop, and it's divine – after being on a very low budget this kind of breakfast is pure heaven, eggs, bacon, beans, sausage, the whole works – three months' of breakfast abstinence on one plate – sheer heaven.

After breakfast is over and done with, we ventured back to our room. We see that the weather has changed, the mist has lifted, and the mizzle abated, strands of blue sky appear in between the grey clouds – after all, it is the 1st October, the beginning of Autumn. I'm wanting to take a quick walk up to The Mariners Church – St Ives Society of Artists to say goodbye to April, the gallery manager, and to buy a few of their cloth shopping bags which will make lovely presents to take back. When I arrive at the gallery, there is no April and only one bag left, which I purchase from a besuited gentleman who looks more like he should be working in a solicitor's office.

My last day in St Ives, and after buying a few small

boxes of Cornish Clotted Cream Fudge, to replace the lack of bags for presents, we decide to do a circumnavigation of the mediaeval town walking along the beach, and through the ocean wherever we wish. That's what I love doing most, and I am grateful that the day is allowing for this, as the clouds have lifted and there's a clear blue sky above. Walking along the shoreline, barefooted deep in the cool, clear water as the waves splash gently against my legs, I find myself thinking about the last three months of my spiritual journey here to St Ives, and what this journey has meant.

Discovering and getting to know a town that I lived in for seven years in the 1960s, at an age when life is full and exciting, and your surroundings mean little . . . has been high on my list. Quite frankly, I believe there are not too many creaks, crannies and cobblestones left that I've not trodden upon in my search for St Ives. Meeting up with a few old friends from those far off days has been a great bonus, and I thank St Nicholas, each time I visit his medieval chapel (once used by smugglers) perched on top of the Island . . . that there are a few of us left.

By chance rather than design, I've made some new friends too. Poet, painter and librettist, Bob Devereaux, photographer, John Chard, artists Judy Symons and Angela Barron, John Morris of Dean Leather Craft, who repaired a leather bracelet I'd bought in the Kruger National Park, shortly before I left South Africa. I met such interesting people like Toni Carver, editor of, The St Ives Times & Echo. We discovered that Toni's wife and I both worked at *The Garrack Hotel* during the '60s. I worked in the still room washing up in the evenings and the weekends to save up for a car – being the only part-time member of staff to stay the entire summer. When it was time for me to leave, the owner of the hotel, John Kilby, handed me a sealed envelope, saying this is a bonus for staying the whole season – dumbfounded, I tore open the envelope to find seventy crisp pound notes inside. Wow! Was I thrilled? £70 in the '60s was a huge amount of money for a washing-up bonus, equivalent today of approximately £1530. Thanking the Kilby's and the full-time staff who were staying, I hot-footed out of The Garrack, back to the bed-sitter to count my savings and my blessings. Putting the hard-earned monies together made it possible to purchase my very first car – a Mini Van, commonly known as the Passion Wagon.

Reminiscing aside, water-walking over, I went to bid the butcher, the baker, and the best pasty maker farewell, and it was hard, really hard. One very last indulgence was called upon as we reached the Wharf – a Moomaid of Zennor 'Shipwreck' ice cream – so delicious I wanted to cry. I think we did the legendary Moomaid's of Zennor, Daisy, Primrose and Sid Vicious . . . proud during our sojourn in Cornwall. Getting back to the Sloop Inn for our last night, we washed, changed, and booked taxis for the following morning to take us to the train station. We'd planned on having dinner at one of the good restaurants that last evening, but when it actually arrived neither of us felt like it, especially after having eaten a 'Shipwreck' with a dollop of clotted cream on top. Instead, we plumped for a modest helping of fish and chips, and a bottle of wine in our room overlooking the harbour. It could not have been better.

A big hug for Annie and fond farewells to the staff in The Sloop Inn who we've only just met, but have been kind to us in our very short stay. Susan departs and waves as the taxi zips her off to the station. The owner of The Sloop, Maurice Symons, sees my travel bags in the small reception office and offers to carry them out to the front of the Sloop ready for my taxi arriving – I tell him that I knew his late father, Henry Symons, who owned the plumber's shop in Market Place and regaled him with the story of Boots Redgrave driving into the shop window in her Mini when the dog in the car with her sprang across knocking her arms from the steering wheel, on spotting another dog in the road. Symons shop window was right royally smashed and Boot's car badly damaged but nobody getting hurt – became the talking point of St Ives for months. Maurice Symons seemed to like hearing this story told at first-hand, whereupon my taxi arrived and whisked me deftly away to catch the train to Heathrow for my flight home to South Africa and the beautiful wildlife.

Chapter Four

St Ives 1963

Olive Falls, my flatmate, told me that she was going away on holiday to Cornwall, and asked me if I might like to join her. In her lilting Irish accent, she suggested a two week holiday in St Ives, and handed me a brochure to look at, which I leafed through and saw that St Ives looked incredible, with small, narrow lanes, a harbour, quaint shops and inns, beaches with white sand, and sea that looked blue, not grey like Blackpool. This came a bit out of the blue and was unexpected. I had never been on holiday other than with my parents to the Isle of Man, Bispham, Cleveleys and Blackpool. Aged thirteen, I had been invited by my best friend at the time, Rhona, together with her parents and brother to join them on a holiday to Newquay. Much to my surprise, my father and stepmother did allow me to go, and I happily joined the Berry family on an epic journey all the way down South to Cornwall.

And it was an epic journey, believe me. On a coach, all the way from central Manchester to Newquay seemed to take forever, and poor old Roy, Rhona's brother, had to sit next to someone he didn't know, there being five of us, we younger ones swapped seats until we arrived at our destination slightly fractious but dead excited. To me, it was like landing on another planet. The whole of Newquay felt light, bright and sunny. With pavements teeming with good-looking people, we made our way to the Harbour Hotel, where we were booked on a special. Set on a cliff above the harbour, with the glittering blue ocean below, The Harbour Hotel was the poshest looking place I had ever seen. We spent a great holiday together that week during which time Rhona and myself cemented a firm friendship. I fell in love for the very first time in Newquay, with a blonde-haired, blue-eyed boy who looked like Troy Donahue, and I was in heaven, spending time on Fistral Beach, swimming and surfing. Discovering that we could buy a pack of Domino cigarettes – five small affordable cigarettes at a tobacco shop seemed to have been a highlight for us then. Accepting Olive's invitation, we set to and made plans.

St Ives was my destiny; I knew that the moment Olive and I stepped off the train that summer holiday in 1963. I felt that I would love it passionately from that moment on.

We found a taxi on the little slip road by the railway station and got ourselves a handsome rogue Cornishman with an accent thicker than pea soup, to take us to the Kynance Guest House. I gazed in awe as the driver obviously took us the scenic route and traversed St Ives from every angle. I was smitten. The quaint Cornish fishing village captivated me completely. It was so unlike anywhere I had ever seen apart from Newquay. Blackpool, Cleveleys, Bispham – these places had been our holiday destinations and hotspots as a family. Grey sky, grey sea, grey sand, and rain.

This is fantastic, I kept telling Olive as the car wound its way along a very narrow street and down onto the little harbour, sitting there pretty as a picture with its smattering of fishing boats bobbing on the water and a bench where a few old weathered fisherman sat chatting away next to the slipway. Warm sunny skies abounded, and casually dressed people strolled leisurely along the harbour front. Kynance Guest House was up a narrow lane called The Warren, and it was charming.

In fact, it was not a stone's throw away from the railway station but not accessible by car because it is too narrow. Steep steps leading up from the guest house take you directly to the bus station and The Terrace above, which leads to the railway station. Walking there with our suitcases would have been a mission, though I was to climb those steps on many occasions during our two weeks stay there. With exciting anticipation, we showered, unpacked and changed into appropriate holiday clothes – shorts, t-shirts, a gay abandon of colourful, casual, and exciting outfits. Taking our newly-bought bathing costumes and towels, we went out to explore the narrow lanes, cobbled passages, shops, and beaches that made up this little piece of paradise.

Virgin Street, Salubrious Place, The Digey were just some of the names we came across in our meander through the lanes, the steps, and alleyways of fishermen's cottages full of character and charm, each and every one of them. Shops bursting at the seams with tourists, windows full of Cornish pasties, freshly baked bread and saffron cake, their smells permeating Fore Street as we strolled along breathing in everything around us. "This has to be something else," I found myself exclaiming as we came upon Porthmeor Beach – never in my wildest dreams could such a beach exist with its pale blonde sand and turquoise blue sea. The bodies on the beach didn't look too bad, either.

We found a nice spot and spread out our towels, doffed our clothes and covered ourselves in Ambre Solaire sun oil before racing each other down to the water's edge and throwing ourselves with gay abandon into the very cold sea. Neither of us wanted to look as if we were tourists, so dizzying about with toes, ankles, and legs into the water first was out. What a price to pay for vanity – I learned to swim when I was three years old in Radcliffe Baths and have loved the water ever since – but throwing yourself, without any preamble, into the very cold Atlantic waves, was the stuff of madness. Both Olive and I got a tremendous shock at how cold the water was. Lesson learned we didn't do that again in a hurry.

The magic of St Ives captivated us completely; we swam, sunbathed, visited art galleries, potteries, and ate in the numerous coffee shops and restaurants. We explored and came upon old working sail lofts, delved into every nook and cranny of the artistic and enchanting little town like two Alice's in Wonderland. During our holiday, the sex scandal between John Profumo, Christine Keeler, Mandy Rice-Davies and Stephen Ward exploded across the country and became headline news in almost every Sunday and daily tabloid. Our books were abandoned, as reading time became a habit of going to the beach each morning with the newspapers and devouring every morsel of the juicy scandal we could find. In our peculiar society, we get excited when ministers and other public figures are caught with their pants down. In this 1963 scandal, the very notion was deeply, deliciously shocking.

It was at the Copper Kettle Coffee Bar that I met Patrick, a local Cornish farmer. He was tall, wearing tweeds and brogues, had a stutter and played a mean game of squash. He seemed totally out of context in St Ives – which was bordering on the beatnik era and about to erupt into its Flower Power period. My Cornish farmer did not fit in. Patrick was nice, and so started a holiday romance. On our first date, he took me to Tregenna Castle to watch him play squash with a friend. This was the first time I had heard of the game, let alone watch it being played. After showering and changing, he did take me out to dinner. Patrick was not exactly the Australian life-saving hunks we saw on the beach and ogled after, but there was an innocent charm about him which I liked. Olive had met someone she knew from Ireland.

I wish that I could indulge some passion for the romance with Patrick, but it was not like that. No star-lit skies and dark sandy beaches where groups of hippies met and played their haunting guitars well into the night. It was a polite relationship, and Patrick was a gentleman, boring as that seemed at the time. On our last evening together, sitting in his car, he did profess his attraction to me and presented a box of After Eight chocolates as a parting gift. I was duly impressed, having never seen such a box of very thin, delicately square chocolates before, and presumed that they must have been expensive. With goodnight embraces and kisses, taking in the clean, fresh smell of Patrick's neck, we promised letters and phone calls to each other, fully aware that they were empty words.

Sitting forlornly on the train taking us back to Manchester, the holiday over, and reality loomed. Out of the blue, I blurted out to Olive that I was going to go and live in St Ives, whereupon her head shot up from the book she was reading and gave me a look of incredulity and asked me to repeat what I'd just said. "I'm going to give everything up in Manchester and go to live in St Ives. It will take about six months, but I want to live in beautiful Cornwall, away from the North where it always seems cold, grey and miserably wet. Live somewhere warm with blue skies and palm trees," I told her.

Olive gave me a withering look and announced that I was mad to give up accountancy, my good position – to do what in St Ives? Life's too short. I want to live amongst people who write poetry, painters, potters, writers like D.H. Lawrence, who once lived in Zennor out on the coast road between St Ives and Lands' End.

Declaring me totally bonkers, Olive returned to her engrossing book mumbling something about me changing my mind once we got back and settled down into a mundane routine in Manchester, these notions of mine will fly out of the window, soon forgotten. There you go, mundane! I remonstrated indignantly. That's exactly why I want to move to Cornwall. My life at the moment is mundane. If I have to live and carve out a career, why not do it in beautiful surroundings. Olive looked up and gave me a disparaging look, then promptly returned to her book.

On Monday morning, my first day back at Doniger's after the holiday, I give them six months' notice which, I thought, was the correct thing to do. This gave them plenty of time to appoint someone else to fill my position as Head of Accounts, and it gives me time to plan my return and start a new life in Cornwall. The family were taken aback on hearing my news and not exactly encouraging. Auntie Doris was fraught with worry as to what I would do for work in St Ives; a white lie came in here, and I told her that I would be doing accounts for a pottery, to ease her mind. Brenda and Geoff, my older siblings, were busy with their own lives and children; they thought my move to Cornwall was a good idea.

In the meantime, I wrote off to several places to try and get some employment, it did not matter to me what it was as long as I earned enough to get by on. An advert in The Cornishman Newspaper I'd brought back with me caught my eye. 'Manageress/waitress required for the season 1964, starting April – September, accommodation included. Please apply in writing to: The Copper Kettle, Wharf Road, St Ives, Cornwall' – the very place where I had met Patrick. This would be perfect and I duly wrote off for the position.

The following March, I arrived in St Ives on a cold stormy day, and it was not the St Ives we had left the previous summer. My spirits dropped as I stepped from the train and battled my way in the pouring rain along the wharf to the Copper Kettle, a coffee bar and afternoon tea restaurant, one of St Ives' oldest and well-know with a lovely view across the harbour. I had been summoned to start in March in order to get the Copper Kettle ready for the season. What a great place it was. The owners, Henry and Joan, from a well-known Cornish family, lived on the premises and had two sons, John and Robert. Robert was my age, and we got on famously. My accommodation was a small clean, perfectly adequate room above the restaurant itself, and very cosy. I was shown all the ropes and pretended to be quite knowledgeable, managing to take on the persona of having worked in the hospitality business before, which I had not.

Some days, Henry and Joan went and spent the night at their house in Lelant, leaving Robert and me to our own devices, which usually ended up with us going to the Sloop Inn for a drink and a pasty. It was in the Sloop that I tasted my very first beer. I listened to what other people were ordering then asked for a half of bitter, nearly spitting it out after the first gulp. After an evening in the Sloop, we would go back to the Copper Kettle. Pop Short, Robert's grandfather, kept a wonderful wine cellar there and Robert would raid it on more evenings than I care to remember when he was three sheets to the wind, glugging it from the neck of the bottle sitting at the kitchen table. One memorable evening, he performed this same ritual creeping down to the cellar and returning with a bottle which he opened, took one mighty mouthful then spat it out in horror. Father or grandfather had cottoned on to Robert's wine pilfering and caught him out by urinating into a few empty bottles, re-corked; they left them in a convenient place. I laughed all the way to bed that evening. Robert never took another bottle.

The season was balmy, and I savoured every minute. Managing, waitressing and coffee maker was immensely hard work, but I took to it like a duck to water. Meeting lots of people, tourists and locals was fascinating, and I became an entertainer, revelling in the holiday mood, and chatting to people who came back time and time again. I had one full day off a week and a couple of hours during each day depending on shifts. By myself or with one of my new local friends, this precious time off would be spent on Porthmeor or the Harbour Beach, sunbathing and swimming . . . idyllic.

Robert announced to me one morning after we'd been for a drink in the Sloop the night before, that Seth, who he'd introduced me to, thought I was handsome. I responded by telling Robert, that I was a woman and the term handsome, is usually referring to a man. He soon explained that, "the term 'ansome' is a Cornish expression for liking you – so I'm telling you that Seth likes you."

After responding to Robert by saying Seth should ask me himself, and I didn't want to go out with a smelly Cornish fisherman who looks like a Spanish pirate and smokes Gauloises. A few days later, Seth did ask me out and we went for a drink, and then on to the best fish and chip restaurant behind the Sloop, which was delicious. I romanced for a while with my rough Cornish fisherman who already looked as if he was steeped in history. Groping in the sand dunes on a dark night was Seth's idea of a date, but I enjoyed the ride while it lasted, the memory reminding me of a long lost era of pirates and wenches.

The Copper Kettle closed at the end of September for the season and would not re-open its doors until the following April. It had been a great experience, and I would miss the wonderful smell of fresh coffee, the baking of scones and I earned enough money in wages and tips to buy me some time for several weeks. An amazing change descended over St Ives once the season had finished, as it transformed itself back into a small local village again. Darker nights and cold weather set in, and the atmosphere took on a completely different feel. One or two little cafés remained open along the seafront and we locals, as I now classed myself, often met up for coffee, cheese on toast with crispy bacon at an Italian café called Luca's, on the wharf, dressed in the fashionable attire of the time, a fisherman's sweater and Levi jeans, to discuss art, literature, Freud and Jung – such wise philosophers all of us. Luca's was where I first met Patrick and Delia Heron, who were sitting at a nearby table, dressed in the same fisherman's sweaters like mine – in fact Luca's was just a spit away from the Fisherman's Co-op, where most of our clothes were purchased, fisherman's smocks, sweaters – Guernsey's, Aran's and wet weather gear.

There was no work to be had in those first, end of season weeks, so we had to resort to signing on the dole to make ends meet. Nothing could have felt colder. Continuous drizzling rain created a damp and misty atmosphere. Cornwall in November after a halcyon summer was not the same place. Grey and depressed seasonal workers shuffled half-heartedly into the employment office, hoping upon hope that the aficionados sitting, equally as miserable with pursed lips behind the counter, would not find them a vestige of work. But instead, they produced a small amount of cash at the end of the week to keep body, soul, and roll-ups together.

A motley crew the lot of us, our spirits were willing but our minds on another planet. We had to get through this winter season, stick it out somehow without having to return to our homes in Manchester, London, Birmingham, Bradford . . . that would never have done. St Ives was going through a transitional period, and we just had to be there. It was the tail end of the beatnik period, and we were entering into the hippie and glorious Age of Aquarius . . . Flower Power era!

There was a scruffy black duffle coat ahead of me in the queue, hood down revealing long blonde hair, a tad limp and straggly. This sort of person needs the money more than I do I thought to myself guiltily, though why I should be feeling guilty, I had no idea. I'd worked dutifully for the season at the Copper Kettle tea rooms on the seafront with a room thrown in – an entire season, in fact, something that not many aspired to, but I managed and saved what little I could out of the meagre wages and a load of tips. Notwithstanding kitting myself out in the local garb and going to the Sloop Inn almost every night of the week for a half of bitter trying to feel like a local, I might have been . . . well off.

What was it about that black duffle coat, or was it navy blue? That so drew my attention. As if on cue, the figure unhurriedly sauntered out of the line of people before even getting to the counter and left the building licking a Rizla paper round a thin line of tobacco. She looked such an interesting character, very much like everyone else in that room other than exuding an eerie presence, not belonging, but strangely detached, in another world.

There was no getting away from work, and by that time, as February approached, I personally didn't want to. It was proving to be a long winter, and I was not a shirker. Daffodil picking entered my life on a freezing cold February morning, on a farm somewhere near Godolphin. It was piece work and you were paid by how many bunches of daffodils that you picked per week. The first morning, we all gathered together in one of the flower sheds. We were told to change into our oilskins and wellingtons and then asked to wait around in a field until the frost had melted from the stems of the daffodils, whereupon we could proceed in picking.

All steam ahead, sun out, sap defrosted, we set to. It became a tour de force from that moment about who could pick the most flowers in a day. Of course, we out-workers were ostracised by the permanent flower-pickers, the strong local Cornish lasses looked down on us, even in the canteen shed we were divided like North and South. The first evening at home after a long days picking, found me bent double, and I could not straighten up, in fact, it took until the end of the first week, after many soaks in the bath and a weekend's rest, before I could stand up straight again. After that, it became a doddle, and the race for flower picking supremacy was on. It was an amazing time, six to eight weeks in all, and we seemed to make tons of money. The local farm pickers softened toward us and even started to admire our relentless dedication. Of course, quite a few pulled out due to backache, frostbite and a warm bed, but the core of us battled on until not one daffodil was left standing.

A new season is about to be upon us and I'm approached to work in a new coffee bar, the Sugar 'n' Spice in St Andrews Street. This is the real McCoy despite the rather sweet and inappropriate name. Zoe, the owner, comes from Scotland, and I don't think she'd quite grasped the gist of St Ives in the 1960s, artists, potters, sculptors, flower people and pot. But the thought of a new Gaggia coffee machine with a powerful steamer waiting to be thrown into life capped it for me, and the job was mine. Zoe baked the most amazing large chocolate and coffee cakes imaginable, she did this in the flat above, supplying the Sugar 'n' Spice with these superbly delicious confections at an alarming rate, otherwise, she kept out of the place and left me to manage it.

The Sugar 'n' Spice Coffee Bar became the "In" place to go, despite its name and the rather conventional round tea-room tables and chairs. The local community flocked there in droves, surfers, painters, beatniks, and tourists alike. I think the cake did it, Zoe couldn't make the cakes quick enough, and along with good coffee, some great folk music, and a packed café buzz, the place simply took off.

Folk singer Donovan along with his good friend, Gypsy Dave, graced the Sugar 'n' Spice quite frequently, and this set another kind of trend – the folk music followers and marijuana. It was all good fun and relatively harmless, and one had to believe and hope that nothing was smoked on the premises. One morning, I looked up from my beloved Gaggia – which was constantly on the go, even with its four percolation heads it was difficult to keep up with the demand – and there stood the familiar black duffle coat ordering a coffee and a slice of chocolate cake. The face was wan and waif-like with pale brown eyes and my immediate thought was, '*I wonder if she can afford it.*'

The black duffle coat became a regular at the Sugar 'n' Spice, until I realised this was happening quite frequently and nearly always when I was alone, nearer and nearer to closing time at 5.30 p.m. after the staff had left. She appeared to know quite a few of the people who inhabited the cafe but never actually took her coffee and sat with them. I gathered from picking up dog-ends of conversation that her name was Betty, she confirmed this herself one day when giving her order over the counter. "Oh, by the way, my name is Betty," she announced.

As the season moved on everyone was in the full thrall of Flower Power, the throngs went around with flowers in their hair, wearing flowing coloured skirts, Indian blouses, and brightly coloured trousers, with the odd pair of jeans thrown in. You name it, they all wore it, even the Australian life guards-cum-surfers on Porthmeor Beach threw themselves and their bodies into it as St Ives rocked and bathed in peace and love. Although I embraced it and revelled with the rest, my reserve kicked in and apart from the odd flower here and there my dress remained Levi's or shorts and a t-shirt, with the odd Indian blouse thrown on to show I was one of the crowd – especially for a party.

The memorable opening of the Revolution Boutique in Island Square took a lot of beating for claim-to-fame. This was a partnership between Caroline Illsley and Owen Olver. It brought a little bit of swinging London and current fashion to Cornwall amid a blaze of fury by some of the locals when Owen painted 'Revolution' in large red block letters on the side of the new shop. He was just about to add 'Boutique' underneath when TV camera crews descended upon them and large groups of people gathered shouting "Communists", until Owen explained to one camera that 'Revolution' was not a political word as far as he was concerned. It was only the name of a shop for God's sake – whereupon the camera crews and non-locals adjourned to The Sloop Inn, and a good time was had by all. The Boutique got maximum publicity and did very well.

Mr. Peggotty's, the first-ever St Ives disco was welcomed with open arms (well, welcomed by some), now there was somewhere to hang out and to dance other than the round of parties in people's cramped homes fuelled with wacky baccy and unfermented sake´. The beatnik and hippy-favoured beaches; Porthmeor and the Harbour were often too cold and too damp for a night of "going to San Francisco with flowers in your hair". A new discotheque in the back streets of St Ives amid old sail lofts and fishermen's cottages drew the people in swarms that brought its own trouble, especially in the wee small hours and closing time. On the whole, Mr. Peggotty's sorted the wheat from the chaff of unsteady rabble-rousers and St Ives had a well-known and much loved discotheque in Porthmeor Road that would last for many years.

After the first flushes of the Revolution Boutique,

Owen went on to open the iconic Outrigger Restaurant with his partner, Rob Brown. A short distance away from the Sugar 'n' Spice on the corner of St Andrews and Street-An-Pol, the Outrigger became as popular in the evenings as the Sugar 'n' Spice was during the day but with a slightly different clientele. Dining here you were more likely to find well-known local artists such as the sculptor John Milne, The potter's, Bernard and Janet Leach, Brian Smith (Barbara Hepworth's personal assistant), painters, Wilhelmina Barnes Graham, Patrick Heron, Douglas Portway, these were the doyens of successful contemporary artists exhibiting and members of the Penwith Society of Arts whose work was on permanent display at the Penwith Gallery. These were the artists earning good money from their work. Let's not forget the all-important holidaymakers who also thronged to the Outrigger. The white-skinned, over-sun-burnt – dressed like a clod – holidaymaker who, after all, kept alive the St Ives restaurants, pubs, guest houses, pasty and cream tea suppliers, gift shops, and art galleries.

Betty was lingering in the Sugar 'n' Spice one afternoon near closing time looking down-at-heel and unhappy. "I'm really teed off with washing up and working at that grotty café," she announced, while sitting on a stool at the counter draining the last remnants of her coffee. I wasn't quite sure which grotty café she meant, and not the least bit interested enough to ask. "Sharing a house in Bowling Green Terrace with Martin Val Baker and a few drop-outs isn't exactly working either, and I don't have any money to get out of St Ives, I need to go back to London. It'll be the end of another season soon, and then there will be no jobs at all, and it'll be back on the dole." Betty muttered on depressingly.

At that point in our non-existent friendship, she would wait until I finished work and then walk back with me to the door of my bedsitter at the top of Academy Steps. We exchanged goodbyes until the next day when the same routine would happen again. It never dawned upon me to ask why she continuously did this, it evolved of its own accord, and to me, it was rather like having a side-kick. We sometimes found ourselves together at the same party where she would follow me home, even if I was with someone else.

It became irritating in the end. Although I found Betty very interesting to talk to, and we had some really good discussions, it was like having a shadow following me around, turning up out of nowhere wherever I went, and after work, she would be there each and every day. We were in essence, light years apart, from different backgrounds, upbringing, North and South, Labour, and Conservative. I sincerely was the epitome of everything Betty was opposed to in a human being, but there again that might have been the attraction.

Whatever was going on with Betty was beginning to wear thin with me, so seizing the opportunity as she sat at the Sugar 'n' Spice counter one afternoon feeling sorry for herself. "I'll pay your train fare if you want to go back to London," I told her, probably a tad too enthusiastically. Betty's doleful eyes shot up, and I almost detected a spark in them. Betty remonstrated by shaking her head and saying she could not take my money. But the die was cast; my determination was greater than hers, as I handed over the money for a train ticket from St Ives to London.

Life without the perpetual duffle coat beside me felt rather empty. Rejoicing on the one hand at the release, but on the other hand, the incredible limpet had made its mark, and I felt myself missing the companionship and, more interestingly, the intelligent conversation. We were living in a frivolous time capsule, the sixties were ours, hippies, drop-outs, flower-people intermingled with artists, writers, and intellectuals – I personally thought myself a philosopher . . . how crazy was that? But no deep conversations were had between the lot of us as we drifted from work to party, back to work (if we were up in time), off to party again, drinking cheap red wine and the ever-present, home-brewed sake´ – no-one ever let it sit long enough to ferment. Addled brains abounded, glorious uncertainty was our future. We were in love with it all.

Going to the bakery up Tregenna Hill late one afternoon, about five days after Betty's departure to London, I spotted a familiar figure quite some way away walking towards me. *No*, I thought to myself, *it can't be*, but as the gap closed between us I knew that it was. Betty had returned, or, she might not have gone in the first place. Upon seeing me, she gave a surreptitious wave of acknowledgment, no hurry, no joyous sense of return. *Well, that was a waste of a few well-earned quid*, I mumbled to myself as the bakery door was about to shut in my face – coming out of the shop, Betty was standing there waiting. I asked her what she was doing back in St Ives so soon.

"I didn't like London. St Ives is much nicer to live in, and I missed you. The light and the vibrancy down here is crystal clear and so much better for the soul, I more or less went, turned around, and came back. You don't look too pleased to see me."

Swallowing the urge to ask about the cost of the train fare to me and the fact that it was meant to be a one-way ticket, I merely said, "hello and welcome back," but refrained from adding, "please, don't keep coming to the Sugar 'n' Spice every day." Fortunately my lack of enthusiasm at Betty's return must have shown and she did indeed, stop haunting the coffee bar on such a frequent basis as she had done before.

Chapter Five

Catch The Wind

Another season came to an end and with it, the long drudgery into winter hung over us like the sword of Damocles. This, of course, was the time in which we could try our hand at pottery or jewellery-making, a time in which to become a great artist, a brilliant writer, or a romantic poet. The time and the resources were all there for the taking. St Ives abounded with people already proficient in these fields and in some cases being willing to take on an apprentice or to give classes.

I took the opportunity of a workshop being offered by a well-known St Ives jeweller in a converted storeroom out at a cottage in Nancledra. Betty, I was to learn, took herself and a girlfriend off to live by the tidal estuary at Hayle Causeway. Our lives and the flower power scene were slowly drifting apart and hardliners like me refused to be shoe-horned out of Cornwall just because it was winter. If you wanted to be classed as a local, then you did not leave St Ives in its hour of need. Pubs like The Sloop and The Castle needed to be refuelled, and the pasty shops kept open, so you just had to get out and find work in whatever form it took. And believe me, we did, from dishwashing to bar work, flower picking to chambermaid, cleaner to waitress, you name it, we did it.

One day returning to my Academy Steps bed-sit, I found a note from Betty pushed under the door. It was an invitation to visit her at the bungalow on the estuary, and it went on to explain that she had a friend visiting from London and she wanted me to meet her. This was interesting as our paths hadn't crossed for some months, and I did wonder from time to time, what was happening with Betty. St Ives, like most small towns and villages, was a hotbed of gossip and you learn very quickly to take whatever you hear with a pinch of salt or ignore completely. Rumours abounded about all of us really, but Betty, being out on the perimeter of St Ives became a sitting target for the gossip of sinister goings-on, smoking dope, all-night parties, and dreamily hallucinating to the music of Bob Dylan et al. But I never took a scrap of notice what anyone said about her, it was speculation or jealousy motivated and like everything in those hazy, crazy days . . . high on emotion.

We met at the bungalow for coffee as arranged, where Betty introduced me to her new friend, Liz Kellett, and to Liz's old school friend, Jane Relf, the younger sister of ex-Yardbirds singer, Keith Relf, who was down on a visit from London. What nice people they turned out to be. Jane exuded a 'fresh from London' air about her and looked good with smooth, long blonde hair and Mary Quant dressed, on a lithe petite figure – a far cry from our Cornish drop-out gear. Betty appeared happy with friend Liz, and a life surrounded by the estuary. She had wanted to show me some of her writing, hence the invitation, she eventually reminded us as we sat around chatting about life, London, and the world in general. Liz and Jane were so refreshing to be with I'd almost forgotten that Betty was there.

It would be unfair to say that I understood what I was reading when sitting aside, looking through Betty's journal. Not exactly poems, not quite lyrics and certainly not a story. I was confused and not at all sure what I was supposed to be looking at, other than a symphony of words in a strange scrawl. I knew the writing alright because Betty had dropped me a couple of notes here and there during our Sugar 'n' Spice period. What I can tell you is, the words themselves were beautiful, poetic, and of another world that quite took my breath away. Reading her words felt like rising out of a quagmire into the light. Not really knowing what to say, as there was nothing strung together in the words themselves to make a whole. "You should be a writer," I told her, handing back the journal.

Betty looked sheepishly as she took it from me. "Well, English was the only thing I excelled at in school apart from dabbling with art, so I thought I'd give writing a go," she mumbled, standing on one foot and then the other in a nervous shuffle.

"You need to put something together in a sentence, write a poem or a short story to get you going, you'll soon fall into the swing of it," I suggested, little knowing at the time that this is what she would do.

Betty carried on her life over in Hayle, where she appeared to be content on a certain level. We sort of kept in touch and I truly believed in her talent as a writer, poet or songwriter, whichever manifested itself into her where she was and wanted to be. Something or someone would turn the deeply locked-in key to the psyche of her innermost self. A spiritual and complex person – deeply troubled in many periods of her life, frequently bringing to mind the genius and beauty in the words of Rumi, and having a certain sadness in such poets as Christina Rosetti and Sylvia Plath.

One day, I received another short letter from Betty asking if I would go over to Hayle and have coffee with her. She didn't drive at the time and relied solely on Liz, or someone else to give her a lift wherever she wanted to go. It had been some time since we last met, so I was always up for a jaunt out of St Ives. Their bungalow at Hayle estuary was always welcoming, though I imagined this would be due to Betty's partner rather than to Betty herself, who never appeared to be in good health or to be looking after herself. The smoking and the straggly blonde hair always gave her a wan look, and being slightly on the emaciated side didn't help. But this was Betty, known as, The Cornish Poet, and for whatever reason, I looked forward to seeing her.

Suggesting a stroll down to the water's edge of the estuary got me up, out of the chair in a trice. Hayle estuary is an important feeding and roosting site for migrating birds and of special importance to wintering wildfowl and wading birds. It's a fascinating stretch of water steeped in history, and I felt an urgent need to be released onto it. Betty started to tell me, as we sat by the water, that she might be doing some song writing for Jane and Keith Relf, and their connections with a new rock band that they were forming in London. She handed me a folded sheet of paper saying that she'd written whatever was on the paper, for me. It was a poem called 'Northern Lights' and it was amazing. Beautiful poetic words that really touched me, believing, of course, it was my northern heritage that inspired Betty to write this poem – that's as far as my thinking went.

Whatever! Poem or song I was really quite flattered that anyone would write something like that for me. Betty explained that she was trying out writing the words to some music that had been sent from London; songs and poems, trying to make them fit together with the music. She was finding it difficult, the words flowed alright, but she wasn't a musician – she assured me she'd press on and see what came of it all. "I might use Northern Lights, one day if you don't mind," Betty told me as I was leaving, with the precious song tucked safely in my pocket.

Heather Jameson, lived at Hanter Chy up Richmond Place which formed the rear half of the house, Trewyn. The entrance was most probably where the horses and carriages were kept in a time when people used such methods of transport. But half of Trewyn House had been sold, and this made a comfortable home for Heather and her two teenage children, Peter and Julia. Heather herself seemed to reside permanently in a separate building that might once have been the stables but now housed a larger than life bed where Heather entertained friends, lovers, her children, and Scottie dog . . . MacTavish. She became the doyen of Flower Power and made – from her bed, the most magnificent paper flowers in all shapes and sizes and in box-loads. Owen Olver became her greatest customer and sold many of her flowers as well as donning them himself during this amazing era. In fact, we all wore Heather's flowers, flowers here, there, in our hair and everywhere. It was a magical time.

For me, Heather, who I guessed was in her mid-forties, residing in the stable block drinking wine or champagne with the odd lover in tow was about as far removed from my northern upbringing that you could possibly get. With her rounded figure and radiant smile, the small lucky gap in her teeth, where a long cigarette holder was permanently poised, gave Heather a haughty grandeur. She exuded a wonderful personality, and it was easy to see how men, usually a lot younger than her, fell for her charms. When she did rise from her bed to go out to dinner, nearly always with John Milne, she appeared radiant. We all loved and enjoyed her company.

We brewed sake´ (Japanese rice wine) at Hanter Chy by the bin load. Gary, one of Heather's boyfriends, thought this was his chance to make a fortune by producing sake´ and selling it. However, it was not to be – the hangers-on were all pretty poor and desperate, and the sake´ bin would get raided and be drunk before it had time to ferment – in fact, I never once saw a glass of fermented sake´. Everyone was brewing it as beer, and wine was becoming more expensive. Gary, in desperation, gave up the idea and turned his hand to something else with which to earn a living. I never knew what Peter and Julia thought of their mother's lifestyle – they themselves appeared perfectly normal teenagers surrounded by opinionated and disgruntled writers, poets, painters and potters who frequently hung out at Hanter Chy.

Jackie Van Gelder opened a small shop called Casablanca, next to the Sugar 'n' Spice in St Andrews Street, selling traditional clothes from Morocco. Colourful jellabas, kaftans, embroidered tunics, silk shirts and pants, lots of jewellery, beads, bangles, and belts set off a blaze of colour in this minute shop. But it was perfect, catering for the bohemian, hippie and flower-power cultures that were trending in St Ives at the time. Jackie hit it spot on with the smell of incense flowing out of the open shop door. Of course, everyone who could afford it flocked to the shop to buy a new item of clothing. Apart from the Fisherman's Co-op and Scarab D'or, further up St Andrews Street, there were no other clothes shops in St Ives. I bought myself a silk tunic in a rich shade of orange, with fine embroidery on the sleeves and down the front in the traditional manner. It was quite smart in its way, and I felt good in it. For the odd dining out or going to a party, the silk tunic filled the gambit and was trending with the fashion at the time.

In 1963-4, St Ives was still reeling from a book written by Sven Berlin, The Dark Monarch, A Portrait From Within, published by Galley Press Ltd, London 1962. The book was withdrawn just days after publication in Autumn 1962, following legal action. The Dark Monarch is a 'roman a clef' portrait of the St Ives artist's colony 1949 and 1950, but written retrospectively in 1960. St Ives is depicted as Cuckoo Town. It was a novel written about real life, overlaid with a façade of fiction. The fictitious names in the novel represent real people, and the 'key' is the relationship between the nonfiction and the fiction.

One copy of The Dark Monarch, however, did escape and found its way to Cornwall, and I perchance happened to fall upon it in a cloak and dagger "guard it with your life" promise, not to tell anyone else of its existence. Of course, I didn't tell a soul, just read it quietly in my bedsitter and found the entire book fascinating and compelling. Berlin left Cornwall in 1953, so I never met him. But many of the paragraphs in the book I found highly amusing, such as these . . . . quote:

With the people who came to live in Cuckoo (St Ives) it was quite different. They were like tadpoles who had been lifted from the stagnant pools of the cities, where the light was kept out with algae and fog, to a bright and glittering Aquarius where they started to immediately glow. Their eyes started to appear, their gill-slits started to disappear, and their tails to fall away. This is what people have called the magic of Cuckoo.

I was close to the Cornish. I worked with them on the fields. Trenching a five or six-acre field by hand with a Cornish spade for sowing potatoes, and leaving it like a billiard table at the end of the day, needed skill and stamina, and a love of work which few will remember. I loved work, and I loved the men with whom I worked: for this, they in return loved me. And I did it because I was hungry. I joined in their struggle for survival that had gone on for centuries. I entered their family system. They told me I was one of them, which was as rare a thing as gold in that rugged fist of land punching into the blue, bruised belly of the Atlantic Ocean.

Albert Mantis (Bernhard Leach) prayed in his pottery for the artists in the lower end of the town who were so poor and drank too much. Charon (John Craze), the boatman, died of drink, as he did every night of the week, with no one to pray for him.

I thanked him (John Craze), and went back carrying the drills we had made – hungry. It was thirty-six hours since I had eaten food of any kind. My stomach was screwed up into a ball, and that weakness accompanied a slight pain in the sides and that lightness of head and clarity of mind that only the starving can know. The only time I collapsed was when I had been five days without food in Winter and had to go to bed to conserve strength to go on working.

I ate breakfast at a little pension called St Elmo's (St Christopher's Guesthouse). The meal was free out of the goodness of the owner's heart, and would sometimes have to last me, drunk or sober, for twenty-four hours. In return, I would occasionally leave a small sculpture on the sideboard amongst the banquet of fruit and cornflakes. Not a word was spoken about this arrangement: it went on for years – a quiet and genuine human exchange.

The Great Dump was where the visitors bathed in the sun. A splendid arrangement of visual smells and pungent objects which were an everlasting challenge to the Borough Surveyor and the Sanitary Inspector. They were dying to tidy up and add another building on this location to the fantastic chain of public urinals which wound in and out of the town. And this they eventually achieved. The battle of the concrete karzie was fought with as much ferocity as was Agincourt... unquote.

Without doubt, there are some amusing truths in some of Berlin's quirky way of writing, as in the first quoted paragraph, about the people who came to live in Cuckoo. A convoluted version of what most St Ives locals or resident artists were saying at the time about the flocks of migrants making their way from the northerly cities and towns to "a bright and glittering aquarium" that is called the magic of St Ives.

The Great Dump as it is referred to in the last paragraph, was in fact, a great unsightly dump, that Berlin could see from his home, The Tower, overlooking Porthgwidden Beach. And it was an everlasting challenge to the Borough Surveyor and the Sanitary Inspector to build yet another public urinal to add to the fantastic chain of urinals in the town. I understand totally where Berlin is coming from in this. Town Councils and Borough Surveyors in Cornwall, and especially in St Ives, are a law unto themselves and a force to be reckoned with.

Berlin was a dancer, painter, sculptor, poet, and writer of fiction, biography and autobiography. He was a great admirer of the St Ives primitive painter Alfred Wallis, who died in the Madron workhouse in 1942. On a visit to St Ives in the 1920's, the artists Ben Nicholson and Christopher Wood, chanced upon a reclusive, semi-literate fisherman living in poverty and spending his time, when not reading the family Bible, in painting pictures on odd scraps of board. Berlin spent the war writing the first, and as yet unsurpassed, 1948 biography, Alfred Wallis Primitive. It is the classic study of the life of the retired fisherman-cum-painter whose primitive depictions of boats, harbours and St Ives houses brought him recognition as one of the most original British artists of the twentieth century. It also portrays Alfred Wallis as an exploited genius, a verdict that enraged Nicholson.

The motive of Berlin's book was to vent personal anger over the hypocrisies of an over-close and competitive art colony. The book was withdrawn after four successful libel actions by members of the extended St Ives family. Sven Berlin is now best known for his controversial fictionalised autobiography, The Dark Monarch.

Chapter Six

Nancledra

New Year's Eve and I've been invited by a friend, Carol Bradbury, to go with her to Trevaylor, the home of Boots Redgrave, at Newmill, on the back road two miles from Penzance. Carol tells me that it is invitation only but assures me that Boots will let me in. I don't feel very confident at tagging along with Carol as she doesn't know Boots very well and I don't know her at all. But it's the party of the year, and there will be many well-known artists, writers, poets, and potters. This all means nothing to me. Just the thought of a change to be going out of St Ives to a famous New Year's Eve party was exciting enough in itself.

The party is due to start at 8 p.m. We were given a lift by invited guests and arrive at Trevaylor to a mass of cars parked on either side of the Newmill road and it is dark, very dark. As we enter the main gates and find the entrance to what I can only describe as a glorious-looking Georgian Manor House, all lit up and ready to roll. But there is a queue lining up outside the rear door, and I can see that the door is opened as each guest arrives, and are no doubt being scrutinised by the party's hostess, Boots Redgrave. Being a queue-less person I want to turn and run, this is not my sort of going to a party, then I realised there was no lift back until!

Standing in that queue waiting for entry, pulled every being in my psyche backwards and forwards – but something compelling made me want to get through that door. This was a first for me, having to stand in a queue to get into a party with a monitored closed door seemed preposterous, and I was about to tell Carol indignantly, that I was heading back to St Ives as this was ridiculous, when we found ourselves in front of the door which swung open and we were ushered through by a short, roundish woman with blonde hair and twinkling blue eyes that looked me over like I was an Aberdeen Angus, and before I could utter any form of apology for not being on the invited list, she pushed us on and thanked us for coming.

Bewildered would be putting it mildly. Inside Trevaylor was lovely, the lights, the decorations and the platters of food, and wine spread out was something I had never seen. The atmosphere was warm and friendly, and at once I felt quite at home amongst, what looked like, a hundred or more guests, all laughing and chatting in groups full of bonhomie. I spotted a few familiar faces, Tony O'Malley, some of the Val Baker clan, Patrick and Delia Heron, Francis Bacon, who I believe was staying with the Herons at their home, Eagle's Nest, in Zennor, Jackie Van Gelder – who was living at Trevaylor, Willie Barnes-Graham and many more. It was a who's who of the St Ives art colony and bohemian lifestyle that was encapsulating the West Penwith Peninsula. It was a good party, and we eventually got back to St Ives in the early hours of a brand New Year. A tiny bit the worse for wear, but in the long scheme of things, I was not too bad. Falling into bed, I tried to remember who I had met and chatted to, and promised to get in touch with until I fell into the deepest of sleeps.

A good walk was called for to herald the start of a New Year, so I phoned my friend Brandon Flynn and suggested a walk along the coastal path to Zennor. A few of us often went out to The Tinner's Arms for lunch on a Sunday, usually by car, nothing fancy just a ploughman's, or a pasty, half a pint and a good old natter putting the world in order as usual. If the weather was good, we might walk to Zennor Head, otherwise, we just sat in the pub and talked, or sat in the car listening to BBC radio 'Round The Horn', which everyone loved. But today, I wanted to walk on the scenic coastal path, with the dramatic cliffs overlooking the Atlantic – a precarious walk at the best of times, taking in about six miles of fairly rough terrain.

Brandon didn't exactly jump at the idea, but when I told him I would be going anyway, probably on my own, he thought better of it and decided a good hike would do him good. It was bitterly cold with a clear sky and no rain forecast, so dressed up warm with boots on we'd be fine. We met on Porthmeor Road by the beach. After checking our rucksacks that we'd got essentials, we walked arm-in-arm to Clodgy Point. Brandon was Irish, with a wicked sense of humour, his real love was horses, he loved riding horses – given the chance he would have ridden on horseback along that coast track to Zennor.

However, he was with me and on his two strong legs to walk a good walk. Reaching Clodgy Point, we went straight onto Hor Point then on to find the Trevalgan Stone Circle (The Merry Harvesters) and Pen Enys Point, where, by this time, the going was really tough. Further south of Carn Naun Point we could see The Carracks. The Carracks and Little Carracks are a group of small rocky islands approximately 660 ft offshore. The Little Carracks are between the Carracks and Towednack Quae Head. The largest island in the group is known as Seal Island, home to Atlantic grey seals, dogfish, sea anemones, and other wildlife, and it's quite spectacular seeing it from such a dramatic vantage point. We'd exhausted our coffee supply during our various breaks when the scenery lent itself to just sit and take it all in.

Mussel Point, then looking down on Wicca Pool, up rocks, down rocks looking precariously to Porthzennor Cove and finally one last surge up to Zennor Head. At one point on this trek, I thought death would be an easier option than going on, entirely my own fault for not being an experienced walker. Brandon on the other hand, appeared quite untouched by our exertions, while not exactly bouncing, he was not puffing and panting like I was, as we sat on the rocks at Zennor Head admiring the dramatic, mind-boggling scenery around us. One could imagine The Mermaid of Zennor swimming, before rising out of the sea down below where we sat. Imagine the smugglers hauling their boat and booty onto the minute sandy cove, with caves set between two soaring cliffs that seemed inaccessible either up or down. Being deeply into reading Winston Graham's Poldark books, this scenery was a backdrop for anyone's imagination, as it was the very setting based on his series of Poldark novels.

Brandon snapped me out of my reverie saying the Tinner's would be closed if we didn't make a move on. One more hurdle on the narrow inland path brought us to the village of Zennor and the welcome Tinner's Arms. Zennor never ceased to fascinate me, and I've made a promise to myself that one day I will own a cottage here in this lovely hamlet with the Atlantic Ocean as its backdrop.

It was too cold to sit outside so we ordered our food, took our drinks, and sat by the warm fire snuggled into the corner. I was exhausted, and although he never said so, I'm sure that Brandon was also pretty bushed. We'd only just made the Tinner's before closing time at 2.30 p.m. so we were lucky on that score and lucky it was open on New Year's Day. The truly brave and purist walkers would have done the complete circle, returning to St Ives via the easier route through the farm fields – but this wasn't for us. A one-way ticket and a lift home were our criteria.

It was lovely being in the low-beamed Tinner's, and as the hot soup and warm pasties slowly revived us we began to feel more human. The usual coterie of locals sat on stools at the bar downing their pints together with the landlord and his wife. It was always the same faces sitting on the same seats, while the landlord's wife, on the other side of the bar, sat on hers. But that's the winter in Cornwall, summer would hail a different clientele when the tourists, walkers, and climbers would bevvy at the bar to get served, and bag outside tables the instant someone vacated one.

John Bellaris, Brandon's business partner – they both owned the Outrigger Restaurant before Rob and Owen took it over – drove over to Zennor to give us a lift back to St Ives. As hard as the walk had been physically for me, it had been worth it. Getting into bed that evening with my latest Poldark novel, I was transported back onto that rugged, dramatic, and devastatingly beautiful Cornish coast.

I walked down Fore Street with the intention of visiting the New Craftsman Gallery to set my eyes again on a painting by, Wilhelmina Barnes-Graham, that had caught my eye. Only the price tag had stopped me from purchasing the painting immediately as it was quite an amazing abstract, and I loved the colours – deep indigo with a red circle and a dash of yellow thrown in. Somehow I really wanted that painting. However, parked just a few feet from outside the gallery window was the cutest thing I had ever seen on four wheels, a Mini Moke Jeep.

So over I went to take a look at that instead of the Barnes-Graham painting. It was an open jeep with a folding canopy you pulled over – a bit like a perambulator – the sides were open with no protection. A strange lady with a gnarled American accent (Texan I'm guessing) came up to me and asked if I liked the Mini Moke, I told her that I loved it. She told me she was the owner and if I wanted to take it for a spin some time – then I was welcome to do so. She introduced herself as Janet Leach, the owner of the New Craftsman.

Taken aback, I introduced myself, and told her I was on my way into the gallery but got diverted by the Mini. Janet said that she was doing some work at the New Craftsman the following afternoon and suggested I took the Mini Moke for a drive during that period if I wanted to. Blown away by this generous offer, all I could do was to nod my head and say, thank you, already mentally juggling my shifts at the Sugar 'n' Spice.

Early the following afternoon, the Mini Moke was sitting outside the New Craftsman and I couldn't wait to drive off in it. I met Janet in the gallery, eyed up the Barnes-Graham painting briefly, and then we went outside for a few instructions – which turned out to be practically nothing as the Moke was unbelievably simple. I decided to take the coast road to Perranporth on the way to Newquay, it was picturesque and a nice chance to be out of St Ives. With the wind in my hair and a sense of freedom, my jaunt along the coastal route was balmy. I decided to stop for a quick recce at Portreath before heading off to St Agnes, found a takeaway coffee, admired the beach and its surroundings comparing it to Porthminster and Porthmeor, and couldn't find any comparison. Having a fascination with tin mines, I wanted to take this opportunity of seeing, Wheal Coates, somewhere between Portreath and St Agnes. Not having a map didn't help, but with the kindness of the locals en route (who seemed amused by the Mini Moke), I eventually found my way to Wheal Coates, and I'm so glad that I did.

Sitting high on the rugged cliffs above Chapel Porth Beach near St Agnes, stand the ruins of one of Cornwall's most scenic and iconic mines, Wheal Coates Tin Mine. The most recognisable feature at Wheal Coates is the Towanroath engine house – and on the clifftop above Towanroath engine house stands the remains of the Whim Engine House – seeing this mine ruin was almost too much for me to take in. The wild and beautiful surroundings were beyond anything I had seen before, this was a place that needed time spent to gather in the atmosphere, to respect the miners who once worked here and to honour the miners who had lost their lives. The mine workings are said to be haunted by the ghosts of miners who died while working at Wheal Coates. Back on the road to St Ives, I made a vow to return to Wheal Coates Tin Mine and explore it with the dignity it deserved.

Arriving back at the New Craftsman, Janet Leach was sitting having a coffee with the manager, Michael Hunt. When they asked where I'd been, I told them about visiting Wheal Coates, and they both seemed unusually impressed. It appeared from their perspective that not many people of my age from up country, now living in Cornwall, were the slightest bit interested in the defunct

Cornish tin mines. Putting them straight, I said that to me, the old engine houses and the mine ruins themselves were of great beauty and character on the Cornish landscape. Janet thanked me for the keys and for giving the Moke a good spin and, if I ever wanted to use it again, to give her a ring at the pottery, or pop into the shop if I saw it parked outside or somewhere near, pointing to a slip road towards Anchor House. "Ah, my friend Norman Stocker lives at Anchor House," I told her. "Yes, you're quite right he does, he's a tenant and a friend of mine," drawled the Texan.

The singer Donovan, together with his friend and tour manager, Gypsy Dave Mills, these free-spirited travellers, visited St Ives on a frequent basis and their favourite place to hang-out during the day seemed to be the Sugar 'n' Spice, which did great business for us. They would sit at one of the round tables, perhaps with a couple of friends where Donovan would get out his guitar and sing a few of his songs in that unmistakable voice of his, 'Catch The Wind', 'Mellow Yellow', the songs of the time – a heavy influence from Bob Dylan and Woody Guthrie. This Celtic folk poet of the sixties brought not only folk music; he also introduced psychedelia counterculture-ism to his sound. We were all enamoured with Donovan, with his gentle, summer of love and flower power influence, strumming his guitar and singing 'Catch The Wind' or his rendition of Dylan's 'Lay Lady Lay' and 'Mr. Tambourine Man', that rocked us through many a rainy afternoon. People soon cottoned on to Don and Gyp frequenting the Sugar 'n' Spice, which clearly put us out there as the place to be. Memories of these special times, I know, will remain with me forever.

Further up St Andrew's Street, another coffee bar opened its doors. The Blue Haven was merely a few yards away from the Sugar 'n' Spice, but a completely different kettle of fish with its bare wooden floor boards and scrubbed top tables. It had a beachy vibe with large, open windows overlooking Lambeth Walk, and the ocean where you would often find someone sitting on the window ledge strumming a guitar. Personally, the Blue Haven was my sort of place, and I loved its simplicity, simple fare and the ambience. This was the home of the bare-footed, hand-made leather sandals and flip-flops brigade – chilled out, relaxed and happy. Phil Moran might pop in or Pat Colley from her shop opposite, Owen Olver on his way to the Outrigger, Arthur Caddick, to write another poem, and even Bob Bourne with no money to buy a coffee. But it was a hidey hole for me to write or read in peace, without interruption, with the sound of the waves splashing up against the rocks of Lambeth Walk.

St Ives's cafe and pub society are filled with an amazing assortment of eccentrics and strong personalities, who are working at great art, literature, and music for which they will be remembered. And all the while cavorting and displaying themselves to the often disapproving public gaze of the time. Flamboyance is not necessarily synonymous with empty-headedness, even though British reserve would like to pin it down as just that. To me, it is a great privilege to live amongst such artists, writers, and musicians and I savour every moment spent in their company. Through the good times, and through the bad, and poverty-stricken times, these artists have stayed true to the belief in their art – when the chips are down, keep on creating. A would-be writer and philosopher myself one day, the greatest lesson learnt – the person in front of you is your teacher!

When we could afford it, going to the Scala Cinema in the High Street was a special outing. A group of us would get together and help each other out so that we could all afford a seat to a particular film being shown that we all wanted to see. This wasn't easy and was usually a long wait until the 'right' film came along, but when we did manage it, we made a good night out of the occasion. The Scala Cinema opened at the end of World War 1. It had its own generator, and the auditorium walls were decorated with galleons in full sail. The proscenium was

18ft wide, and there were three dressing rooms, for variety artists. In the late -1920's Cecil Drage acquired the cinema. He introduced 'talkies', utilising the Edibell sound system (later to BTH). Set on the original site of the Queen's Hotel stables this amazing art deco cinema, plumb in the middle of St Ives, was an experience in itself, even if you didn't want to see the film.

It was time for me to get some sort of transport. The freedom of driving off in the Mini Moke had unsettled me. I needed a car but had not the money to even think about it, let alone buy one. It was a friend, Joyce, who told me The Garrack Hotel, where she was working, were desperately looking for someone for their still room – to wash up in the evenings, at weekends and, the pay was good. "Heavens that would be great," I told her. *But Burthallan Lane was quite a hike up from the town to Ayr and the council estate, and could I possibly do this on a regular basis?* Finding myself thinking this, I picked up the Sugar 'n' Spice phone and called The Garrack Hotel and asked for Mr. Kilby. The following day, I went for an interview at The Garrack and was given the job, three evenings a week and alternate weekends. I told Zoe about this second job and she was delighted for me. Probably more thrilled that she didn't have to give me a rise for my longevity at the Sugar 'n' Spice.

Putting mind over matter about the long haul up to Burthallan Lane three nights a week, I put it into my head that it would be excellent exercise that I never seemed to get around to doing in St Ives, apart from the odd walk here and there. Plus my attempts at surfing and, on occasions, swimming. Six months of this would make me healthy, wealthy and perhaps a tad wiser, became my daily motto.

And it was tedious at first, but once finding the short-cuts and getting the odd lift here and there, it soon became as much a part of my weekly routine as working at the Sugar 'n' Spice. The Garrack was a first-class hotel with a head chef, a sous-chef and all that goes with good food and fine dining. Head Chef Don, always known as Chef, was a work of art to watch and learn from, as was sous-chef, Alec, who could whip up choux pastry and make the best eclairs and profiteroles known to man. My job in the still room was good, machines did most of the washing up, and I did what was required by the rest of the kitchen. I thoroughly enjoyed working at The Garrack apart from the long approach through the council estate to Burthallan Lane. The hotel itself was beautiful, sitting in a secluded location with panoramic views of St Ives Bay. Chef and his wife Joan (head waitress), Joyce and her boyfriend, Ray, and sous-chef Alec all became friends, and on occasions, we would all be invited for drinks to Chef's Park home in the hotel grounds.

Like most of the hotels in St Ives, staff would come and go on a daily basis at The Garrack. Partly due to its location and partly due to how temporary holiday staff operates, here one minute, gone the next. A fact of life for many resorts all over the world and hotel staff management's nightmare. But it happens, and when it does, we all have to fill in the gap and get on with it. From these experiences, I learned so much more about the hospitality trade than I could have hoped for. The end of season was upon us, and it was time for me to leave the hotel. Permanent staff, like Chef, Joan and Alec would be staying on to carry the hotel through the winter months.

There was a deep sadness in me about leaving the Garrack, it felt like home, and I would be leaving my beloved family. Mr. Kilby arrived in the kitchens on my last weekend to say goodbye and handed me an envelope, saying this is your week's wages and bonus for staying the season. Opening it, I was taken aback to see what looked like a lot of money inside – counting it I was flabbergasted. Seventy pounds on top of my wages felt like a fortune – a quick calculation with what I had already saved from my job together with this generous bonus meant that I could afford to buy a second-hand car. Overjoyed, I thanked Mr. Kilby, ate the farewell cake and tea provided by Chef and left The Garrack Hotel in tears.

Out of the blue, and quite unexpectedly, I heard of a flat to rent in Talland Road, slightly past the Malakoff, just above The Terrace. The following day, I went to see about the flat, and the owner showed it to me there and then. It was pleasantly larger than my Academy Steps bedsit – this flat, the top floor of a large, privately-owned Victorian house, had a nice-sized sitting-room-cum-kitchen with a separate bedroom and bathroom and a stunning view over the bay to Godrevy Lighthouse. It was a little way out of the centre of town, but there would be parking space outside for a car, which there certainly was not at Academy Steps. Having recently met a new friend from Australia, Judy Grainger, I asked her if she wanted to share this flat, as she herself was in temporary accommodation. Judy said an emphatic yes, to the idea and two weeks later we moved into Talland Road.

Norman Stocker was owed an afternoon off from the Barbara Hepworth foundry studio, and he gave me a lift to Cambourne to check out a couple of vehicles at a garage advertised in the Cornishman that fitted my price range. After a bit of rattle-tattle, a test drive and negotiation, I finally settled on a Mini Van. Perfect size, just the right price and in good working order – we would return at the weekend to collect it once the garage had done the paperwork. Excited beyond words, I couldn't wait to get the Mini and be out on the road. Having settled in, life at the flat was pretty good. Judy had brought her stereo player, so there was music bashing out from time to time – Scott McKenzie's 'San Francisco', was the rage at the time and we played it ad nauseum, along with The Beach Boys, 'Good Vibrations', 'God Only Knows' and 'California Girls', the music of flower power, surfing and sun. Halcyon days spent in St Ives amongst painters, poets, writers and musicians . . . life could not get better.

Taking ownership of the Mini Van was a proud moment in the middle of Cambourne on a Saturday morning. Suddenly, having my own little world wrapped around me was quite overwhelming; driving back to St Ives was pure joy. I'd worked hard, very hard for this, but the sheer pleasure it gave me far outweighed the six months of washing-up. Arriving back at the flat, I suggested to Judy that we went for a drive along the coast road to Zennor – she leapt at the idea and off we went feeling like the world was our oyster.

Living in the bubble of St Ives did not make us oblivious to what was going on in the rest of the country. This was an era in which anything was possible, and nothing was safe; a time when the established order was being challenged, subverted, and ultimately buried. After "The Chatterley" ban in August 1960, Penguin was prosecuted for publishing one of DH Lawrence's lesser works, Lady Chatterley's Lover, notably only for its use of the f-word and some sublimely silly sex scenes. When Penguin was given the go-ahead to publish, the initial print run of 200,000 copies sold out on the day of issue.

The Beatles rise to stardom, and their music being constantly played fascinated me and everybody else, together with Mick Jagger and The Rolling Stones, the music industry was in an explosion of pop culture. John Profumo, secretary of state for war, who is married to the film star, Valerie Hobson, has embarked on a torrid and sordid affair with Christine Keeler, having met at Lord Astor's country mansion of Cliveden. A brief and passionate affair, and tongues began to wag. The Profumo affair was no passing sensation, it all but brought down the Macmillan Government and it almost certainly finished Macmillan himself as prime minister. Shortly after noon on November 22, 1963, President John F. Kennedy was assassinated as he rode with his wife, Jacqueline Kennedy, in an open-topped car – motorcade through Dealey Plaza, Dallas, Texas. The global shock of JFK's assassination could not have been greater. It literally brought the world into stunned disbelief.

Many heated discussions took place either in the pub or in the Cortina café up The Warren or at the Arts Club at the bottom of the Warren. There was an eclectic mixture of Tony O'Malley, Bob Bourne, Arthur Caddick – if he came down from Nancledra, Denys Val Baker – at times, Stephen Church and myself. Starting off as having a coffee together, this strong-minded bunch would soon start on the political bent turning it always to suit each's own political thoughts. In the main, they were friendly and always in good humour, unless someone had a beer too many which turned into unpleasantness. Life beyond St Ives and art was always an excellent topic – the goings-on in the rest of England and abroad were good for everyone. It took their minds off the petty nuances of the small art colony, whose paintings were hanging where, The Penwith Gallery exhibitions – why was so and so's paintings chosen. Who has the right to choose – how did she manage to get on the hanging committee – I'm never going to exhibit there, if they don't have better art on show. Wills Lane, Marjorie Parr Gallery – too exclusive, she'll never sell anything! On and on it went.

There would be a robust conversation, and sometimes crude remarks about the topical newspaper headline gossip about the fall of John Profumo, Christine Keeler, Mandy Rice-Davies and Stephen Ward's sexual circus. Nothing is more deliciously shocking than finding a Cabinet Minister and his cohorts with their pants down. Then the murmurings of English actress-singer Jane Birkin leaving the composer, John Barry, and starting an affair with French actor-songwriter, and eighteen years her senior, Serge Gainsbourg, the former lover of Brigitte Bardot. The song *Je t'aime*, sang by Birkin and Gainsbourg, was recorded shortly into their affair. The song was written by Gainsbourg for Brigitte Bardot, with whom he was besotted. It became an instant hit and hailed as the most erotic song of all time. The duet reached number one in the UK, and number two in Ireland, but was banned from several countries due to its overtly sexual content. It was played endlessly in St Ives.

At the other end of the spectrum, and more

importantly, the Rivonia trial was taking place in South Africa that led to the imprisonment of anti-apartheid revolutionary, Nelson Mandela, and the others among the accused. They were all convicted of sabotage and sentenced to life at the Palace of Justice, Pretoria. Mandela was imprisoned on Robben Island, 8.6 nautical miles off the coast from Cape Town. Everyone was up in arms about the apartheid Government in South Africa. It caused non-stop discussions with friends in the Sloop or the Castle and other pubs in the town. Also, in the various art studios, people gathered in small groups discussing and sorting out the injustices happening in the world at the time.

A favourite place that I enjoyed visiting one or two evenings a month was The Bluffs, at Hayle Towans. This is where different groups played folk and jazz music, some people danced, and others just listened. I first heard Brenda Wootton sing at The Bluffs. A true Cornish folk singer, with a smile and a heart larger than life, made an evening travelling over to Hayle, worthwhile. It was here that I first got a taste for traditional jazz – not a great jazz lover, but some of the jazz musicians performing at The Bluffs were outstanding. We always enjoyed our visits there, returning to St Ives energised and happy. Hearing that Brenda also performed at the Count House Folk Club at Botallack, in the heart of the tin mining country of West Penwith, we made that a new one to try. It was an eccentric venue that drew singers from far and wide, ten miles from Penzance and thirteen miles from St Ives, out on the barren, wild moors scarred by the haunting shadows of ruined engine houses. This was the best find of all these Saturday night gigs when Brenda would perform 'Lamorna', 'Little Eyes', and 'The White Rose'. We were to find out that Brenda was passionate about her Celtic tradition that she often sang in Cornish, and was fluent in the language.

Another haunt was the Hut Theatre, belonging to The Trencrom Revellers Theatre Club. I was introduced to the Theatre Club by Norman Stocker, who was a great friend of Kenneth Quick, who worked at the Leach Pottery. Kenneth was also cousin to William (Bill) Marshall one of the foremost British studio potters of the 20th century, who was Bernard Leach's first apprentice at the Pottery in 1938. Norman took me to see the Hut Theatre and I'm not too sure why he did this. He told me that in 1963, Kenneth had gone off to Japan to work with Shoji Hamada for a while. Just before his planned return later that year, he drowned tragically in a swimming accident. Kenneth Quick had become a highly regarded potter by this time. Somehow, I don't think Norman ever got over Kenneth's death. He spent a lot of time with his friend, Janet Leach, whose home was a flat above the pottery, where they would happily drink themselves into a stupor with whisky, and smoke endless cigarettes. He ended up one evening so drunk that he fell off the balcony at the top of the steps coming out of the flat, and broke what remained of a half amputated leg that he lost during the war.

I feel that Kenneth must have belonged to the Trencrom Revellers Theatre Group, but I can't be sure – Norman never enlightened me about the reason he wanted me to see the Hut Theatre. So when Judy mentioned that we'd been invited to a party at the Trencrom Hut Theatre, it caught my attention but wondered why someone would be throwing a party way out there. I didn't know the people who had invited us, but she seemed to know them and seemed eager to go. Sometimes, I believe the Theatre Group hired out the hut when it wasn't being used to generate much-needed funds to keep themselves and the hut going.

We drove the four and a half miles to the party in the Mini (aka the passion wagon). Reaching Trencrom, I parked out on the perimeter of the hut area, ready for an easy exit. People were milling around, and the music was blasting away – I felt no desire to go inside the hut as I could tell from the partygoers outside that it wasn't quite my scene, and felt immediately out of place. Not Judy's fault, we were, after all, very different people. Helping myself to a drink, I perched on a broken tree trunk and watched people enjoying themselves – quite a habit of mine and no need for small talk.

After the second drink, the novelty of being there and observing was wearing thin, when suddenly some really nice music started filtering through that captured my attention. As I was trying to work out what band it might be, Judy appeared out of nowhere looking for me. I asked her if she knew what the music was, and she told me it was a well-known band called The Doors, and the lead singer was Jim Morrison. This was playing as part of the discotheque music and what I heard so far was good, really good, 'Light my Fire', 'Hello I Love You', rocked out as I made a mental note to watch out for this band, but as the music got into more sombre, 'The End' psychedelic rock my attention waned and I went in search of Judy to tell her that I was leaving.

One day, I was getting petrol at Marine Garage in Trelyon Avenue when, Jack, the husband of my friend, Pat Colley, turned into the garage to get petrol for his car. He noticed me and strolled over, giving the Mini Van a good looking at. Sandy-haired with a broad Yorkshire accent, Jack was a really decent bloke who worked at one of the mines in Camborne – he'd finished work for the day and was on his way home. Patting the top of the Mini he said, should I ever wish to sell the Mini, he would buy it, as he needed it for his work instead of having to use the car. Promising him first refusal and exchanging other pleasantries, he went off home to his rather glamourous wife, Pat.

I was about to take off from the garage when up behind me drove a green open-topped sports car, a Frogeye Sprite, and who should be driving it, but Brandon. Well, was I impressed? I hopped out of the Mini and went to say hello to Brandon, and admire the Sprite, and what a beauty she was. Brandon told me sadly that he was selling the car as it was impractical for the restaurant business; he needed to get something bigger for getting supplies etcetera. My attention was grabbed, and I dared to ask how much he wanted for the Sprite. It was too much for me, that was for sure when he told me. But then he suggested to get what I could for the Mini and pay the balance to him over the next six months – thrilled beyond words at this suggestion, while quickly doing an accounts reckoning, I left Brandon and the Sprite filling up at the garage and made my way to Nancledra to talk to Jack Colley.

Four days later, I was the owner of a Frogeye Sprite, and I couldn't have been happier. Jack gave me exactly what I had paid for the Mini, which I gave to Brandon, who drew up an agreement for the balance of payment on the Sprite over six months. It seemed as if I hadn't had the Mini for five minutes before abandoning it like a discarded lover, for a better model. But my betrayal did not last for too long. With the top down, and the wind in my hair, I drove around in that little Sprite, showing off my prized possession for everyone to see. I even, very stupidly tried to carry my surf board in the open car down to Porthmeor Beach; a mere five minute walk away – how crass could one get.

Sauntering down Fore Street one afternoon, I happened by chance to pop into The Craftsman shop, and there standing behind the counter was Boots Redgrave, of the New Year's Eve party. She recognised me and seemed to know my name. I hadn't seen her in there before and asked if this was a new job or was she helping out, as seeing her there seemed incongruous with the surroundings. Soon put in my place, Boots told me she was in partnership with Janet Leach of the New Craftsman, a couple of doors away.

We chatted for a bit, telling her that I, together with a couple of friends, was thinking of going to London for the weekend and that I was dithering because three of us could not fit in the Sprite and I didn't really want to go by train or worse, travel there by coach. I've no idea why I'm telling this lady – who I do not know from a bar of soap –

all this drivel, but I am, and she appears to be listening, and when she does speak, she suggests that we take her car as she won't be using it at the weekend, and she can always get a lift if she needs to go anywhere. Taken aback, I couldn't be sure if she was just kidding or could somebody really be that kind. But kindness it turned out to be, and we made arrangements for me to collect Boots' car on the Friday morning outside the Craftsman shop. I offered her the Sprite to use, but she declined, saying she doubted she would fit into it.

I took Boot's car and her twinkling blue eyes together with Carol Jackson and Greta, all the way to London. We dropped Greta off near Westminster Cathedral, and Carol and I went to stay at a friend's flat in Kensington Garden Square. It was a great weekend full of Kings Road, Carnaby Street, The Chelsea Kitchen, and Biba's, a refreshing change from the St Ives that we were so embedded in. We met up with our friends, John and Bill, hit the Bayswater Road on Sunday morning with a walk through Hyde Park on Sunday afternoon. It really was lovely seeing flowers in full bloom under a blue sky with people swimming in the cool water of The Serpentine, it looked idyllic.

Moving on to the Bandstand to catch the 4 p.m. performance, we detoured through Rotten Row, a once-fashionable place for upper-class Londoners to be seen horse riding. A must for us was to visit Speakers' Corner, a traditional site for public speeches and debates since the mid 1800's when protests and demonstrations took place, where speakers such as Orwell and Marx have tried to convert the masses. The Sunday soapbox is where London's pseudo-intellectuals congregate. Carol and I had to be sure we wouldn't get on our high horses and join in any debates going on – if we wanted to return to Cornwall on the morrow, as we can be very feisty in debate mode.

All too soon, the weekend was over, and we were heading back to St Ives minus Greta who had decided to stay a bit longer in London. It was Monday and a bright, cheerful day so we made the most of it by returning across Dartmoor, taking the Moretonhampstead road through to Postbridge, stopping at the 19th-century Warren House Inn marooned amid miles of moorland, with a fire that's been burning since 1845 – we ate a ploughman's lunch, finally arriving back in St Ives at 6 p.m. It was a short break for such a long drive but well worth the effort.

Parking Boot's car outside Anchor House the following morning as arranged, I went in search of the kind lady herself to return the keys. Still feeling overwhelmed by this act of generosity, my mind was working overtime, how to repay Boots other than having filled up the petrol tank – flowers, a bottle of wine, whisky or a box of chocolates, all seemed a bit inadequate not knowing the person. She was not at the Craftsman shop when I got there and was told by a lady opening up, that Boots wouldn't be in until later that afternoon. Having to get to work myself, I wrote a quick note of thanks together with the keys, saying I would pop by sometime soon.

Two weeks later, I was passing the Craftsman shop and spotted Boots behind the counter and went in at long last, to thank her personally for the loan of her car. She thanked me for refuelling the car and asked about the trip. It seemed by then, such a long way back that I could barely remember, but made what I did remember, sound interesting, feeling more hell-bent on trying to ascertain something nice that I could do for her in return. The conversation brought the idea itself, after a brief discussion on London restaurants; I suggested to Boots that I took her out for dinner, somewhere in Penzance maybe.

Chapter Seven

Heather Cottage

Jewellery making under the tutelage of Bryan Illsley was coming along well considering our one night a week stints in the little workshop. I really had taken to it like a duck to water, surprisingly. Bryan was encouraging but did not suffer fools gladly. Greta soon got fed up and pulled out, as did Jackie – someone else lost interest after the first workshop and didn't appear again. This left me. Bryan, who works together with, Breon O'Casey, a well-established goldsmith, and jeweller, were making a name for themselves in St Ives at the time and Bryan really couldn't justify working on a one-to-one basis with me as financially it wasn't viable. I felt pretty gutted about this as I'd already invested in some good German jewellery tools, and recently sold a silver necklace and a bracelet to a private customer. Seeing my disappointment, Bryan set up a series of short workshops for me, some at the little workshop and one or two at his and Breon's studio, where, he assured me, I would learn a great deal more with him than I was learning alone. So upbeat and happy with this arrangement, my talents were coming into fruition, and for the first time, it occurred to me that one day, I might well become a jeweller.

    Greta's father, Robin, was a good friend who I frequently visited as he loved to cook, and I in turn loved to eat. This sixty-something-year old man, tall with a whispering of silver hair, was as mischievous as could be. We spent many happy hours together as I just loved his sense of humour. There was no mention of Greta's mother and no mention of Robin's wife. I'd heard murmurs of Greta's mother dying at childbirth but this was never corroborated by either Greta or Robin. Robin's cottage was full of lovely antiques, wineglasses, cutlery, and napkins like remnants from a once grand lifestyle tucked neatly into a Cornish cottage. He bought and sold three properties during the time I'd been in St Ives, each time moving into a smaller home. In hindsight, I think he did this to generate an income, but who cares, Robin was as camp as could be and we spent great times together. It was hard to believe he was ever married, total lack of information from Robin or Greta, nor any discussion on this leads me to believe – something happened way back when, that we will never discover.

I found myself passing the Craftsman shop and the New Craftsman gallery quite frequently, but I never saw Boots in either of the shops. Then one day, out of the blue – there she was arranging something around the counter, giving a cheery wave, she beckoned me in. I got a little remonstration from Ms Redgrave, that I was about to walk past without saying, hello. That was not the case I told her, she had looked busy and pre-occupied and I didn't want to disturb her. She didn't believe me for a moment as those twinkling blue eyes looked straight into mine for a second, making me feel nervous and disconcerted. We chatted for a few minutes, and then she brought up the subject of my offer of taking her out for dinner. At the time that I'd asked her she never responded so I had taken it for granted, the answer was no. Surprised now, I assured her the offer was still there and I would be delighted for us to have dinner together. That was settled, on one condition Boots insisted, that she drove me over to Penzance and bought the dinner.

As arranged, Boots picked me up at Talland Road, in, of all vehicles, the Mini Moke – well that was a surprise, wondering what she was doing with Janet Leach's car. It was soon explained that Boots' car had gone for a service so she borrowed the Mini Moke. Travelling in this vehicle was all very well and good during a warm, sunny day, but this evening was cold and wet, even having the canopy over did nothing to keep out the wind and the driving rain with its open sides, making conversation impossible. I should have insisted on going in the Sprite.

Arriving at The Meadery on Wharf Road, somewhat dishevelled, we rushed inside and found a nice cosy table. I'd never eaten at The Meadery before, so it was a new experience for me, but not quite the type of place I imagined Boots inhabiting, being a family restaurant and a popular one in Penzance. I had clearly got it into my head somewhere more sophisticated but there again; maybe she thought I was The Meadery type. We ordered a bottle of wine, scampi and chips for me, mackerel and salad for Boots and settled down in the candlelit glow and chatted away.

Boots told me that she was once married to the painter and sculptor, William Redgrave, whose studio 3 Porthmeor, was once used for the St Peter's Loft art school that he ran with Peter Lanyon, whose students included Tony O'Malley. Peter Lanyon later used it for his 10m wide painting commission 'Porthmeor'. Boots had two children with William Redgrave, a daughter, Stella and a son, Nicholas. She told me how she was still mourning the death of her beloved friend, Peter Lanyon, who had died from the injuries of a gliding accident in August 1964. She'd adored Peter and was great friends with his wife, Sheila, often visiting her and her six children, at the family home, 'Little Parc Owls' in Carbis Bay. I could see Boots was pretty upset telling me about Peter, but it seemed she needed to get it off her chest and talk about it. He'd been a fine abstract artist, whose work she'd much admired.

I reminded her of the New Year's Eve party at Trevaylor and asked if she remembered me going as an uninvited guest. Boots had remembered me arriving with Carol Bradbury – I was impressed, because she was very fraught at the time keeping unwanted gate-crashers out. She told me that she didn't own Trevaylor, but was in some kind of partnership of the property with her friend, the artist, Nancy Wynne-Jones, who lived in the attractive gate house. Nancy bought Trevaylor in 1962 and turned many of the rooms into studios. It was to provide a stimulating environment for artists and writers to work in and exchange ideas. The poet WS [Sydney] Graham and his wife Nessie lived there, as did the Irish painter Tony O'Malley. Nancy had been especially devastated by the death of Peter Lanyon, but the presence of the painter and sculptor Conor Fallon, provided her with empathy and solace. Nancy was besotted with Conor and about to up sticks and move with him lock, stock and barrel to Kinsale in Ireland, leaving Boots bewildered and without a home as Trevaylor had to be sold and she did not have the kind of money to buy Nancy out. Boots rented a cottage in the village of Nancledra, which is where she was now living.

Fortunately, when we left The Meadery it had stopped raining and we were thankful for that, another cold trip ahead but not nearly as bad as the driving rain. Now fortified with good food and wine we set off for the return journey to St Ives. Still trying to talk, but with great difficulty as the wind blew through the Mini Moke, and just holding on was an effort. I noticed there were now no street lights and realised that we were hurtling forward on a dark country road and not on the main road that we'd travelled from St Ives to Penzance.

Mentioning this to Boots, she seemed pretty startled saying she'd automatically taken the route to her home in Nancledra, now it was too late to turn back. Whatever, this back road would eventually take us to St Ives, albeit via a longer route. Suddenly, the Mini stopped on what felt like a very dark lane but I could make out a light down a small embankment to a cottage nestled there below. Boots told me she felt she couldn't drive any further, and I was welcome to stay at Heather Cottage. My insides turned over at this suggestion, not quite knowing what it meant, so being the coward that I am, I declined the offer and said I would walk back to St Ives. She reminded me it was a long way, but should I change my mind she would leave the door of the cottage unlocked.

It could not have been darker as I set forth along the

narrow lane towards Nancledra village and on to St Ives. No torch, no light and not even the moon or the stars, I had only my obstinacy for company. I felt hugely attracted to Mrs Redgrave, her blue eyes, blonde hair and highly intelligent mind had unnerved me from the first. She was twenty years my senior, short and round, Boots was not a beauty, but her voice, her mind and her presence more than made up for the aesthetics. It was hard to believe that I was standing there in the dark night dithering whether to walk on or to go back. It would be half an hour back and probably two to three hours walking to reach St Ives, unless I got a lift when I hit the main road in the village.

Standing there thinking, nothing was making me go forward so I made the decision to return to Heather Cottage and face whatever fate had in store for me there. Entering the garden gate of the cottage the outside light was still on as I made my way to the kitchen door on the left that Boots had told me she would leave unlocked. A haranguing of barking burst forth as I touched the door handle, making me jump out of my skin as two Bassett hounds burst forth and almost knocked me down. They flew out into the garden as I let myself into the kitchen that was lit up by a small lamp, warmth from the Aga oven and so inviting. I then heard Boots shouting down from upstairs to leave the dogs outside in the garden, lock the door and to come upstairs to bed.

The following morning, Boots brought me coffee in bed, which was – sheer luxury. Looking out onto the garden from the bedroom window was a pleasure. Hearing the birds singing and the dogs barking felt like true country life after St Ives. Heather Cottage sat long and low in a small valley with a pretty rambling garden and a river running through it. An idyllic Cornish granite cottage with its big kitchen and Aga oven, Heather Cottage would be most people's dream of a home in Cornwall. Jackie van Gelder had moved to the cottage with Boots and was busy having an affair with one of the hunky Australian surf lifesavers, called Chris. Jackie's bedroom was directly above the kitchen and accessed by stairs leading up from the kitchen – noisy and prohibitive at times Boots told me, especially first thing in the morning, she said shaking her head distastefully.

Boots gave me a lift back to Talland Road in time for my shift at the Sugar 'n' Spice. We said our goodbyes and made no arrangement to see one another again or even phone. At the flat I was greeted by a hostile Judy asking why I hadn't come home after dinner, or even phoned to say I'd be out for the night. Quite rightly, I should have let her know, but I hadn't. Selfish yes, confused yes, but Judy was not someone I needed to be accountable to. She might have thought so, but she was sorely wrong. The seed was sown and the atmosphere fraught from there-on-in. If she disapproved of my one night relationship with Boots then so be it.

The catalyst to living at Talland Road came in the form of Pam Randle, a friend who needed a place to live for a week or two. We allowed Pam to stay in the sitting room and sleep on the sofa. One evening, while sleeping peacefully in my bed, I heard voices and realised it was Pam returning home but the other voice was that of a man. Judy and I had stipulated she was to bring no-one to the flat during her time with us – but sure as can be, I had heard a man's voice. Not wanting any confrontation at 1 a.m. in the morning, I turned over and tried to go back to sleep. Suddenly the banging started and the flat shook and the floor rattled – leaping out of bed, I rushed to the sitting room door and could hear Pam and a man going at it like hammer and tongs. I froze in horror at such banality, they were obviously having it off on our rush matting floor. Knocking on the door didn't help and without waking the entire house up, I left them to it and went back to bed. The next morning saw no sign of the male she'd dragged home but Pam lay flaked out on the floor. I prodded and poked her awake and told her to get out, and not to return, right now before I left for work. Judy kept out of it but completely agreed that Pam should go, and the sooner, the better.

Staying in the Talland Road flat was never the same after the incident with Pam and I could never quite enjoy eating at the dining table that stood on the rush matting; too close for comfort to the fornicating that had taken place there. The friendly relationship between Judy and me was never quite the same after my night away with Boots, making the atmosphere tense and strained. Time to move on presented itself when one bright sunny day I received a phone call.

My new home became a house called Trewyn. This is perhaps the largest and most beautiful house in the centre of St Ives owned by the artist and sculptor, John Milne. If you had to fall with your bum in the butter, then I fell well into this one. I first met John at the opening of an exhibition held at the Penwith Gallery. It was a marriage of souls on first meeting, and now John was offering me his house to live in – he had a studio at the bottom of his lovely garden, and spent long spells in London, Morocco and other parts of the world. John was a sophisticated man twelve years older than me, and came from Eccles, a suburb of outer Manchester. He was always beautifully dressed in a casual way, with closely cropped blonde hair and a suntanned body. His superb taste in décor, food and art was well known, as was his lovely sense of humour. My role in this would be to keep an eye on the house and if any of his London friends wanted to stay, I would see to it that rooms were ready and breakfast was served. This was a pleasure beyond dreams.

Staying at Trewyn was glorious. John's friends were invariably sophisticated people from all over the world, but mainly from London. There were film directors, actors and actresses, artists and writers. Some were personal friends, others were paying guests. John's partner was an Italian chef and the housekeeper, Ivaldo, who cooked the most delicious dishes imaginable. The music of Mozart, Handel and Puccini always rang through the house. Opera was played and I learned about singers such as Leontyne

Price, Joan Sutherland, and of course, Maria Callas. I was not altogether ignorant of opera as my mother loved Kathleen Ferrier and Paul Robeson with their deep resonant voices, which we heard frequently in our home.

An invitation to have dinner with a table of guests staying at Trewyn culminated in the first sale of my jewellery. It was a long silver necklace of hammered discs I was wearing for the occasion, when one of the ladies asked where I had bought it. I made it myself I told her proudly. She asked if it was for sale or could I make her one. Taking me by surprise, I was about to harp and stutter my way into saying it would take quite some time to make another necklace, when common sense took over in the nick of time. I apologised and explained that each piece of jewellery was individual, designed and made by me. I will not duplicate a design. I can make one similar which will take quite some time, or you can buy this one, I heard myself telling her, trying for the world to sound professional. The lady in question said that they were leaving at the end of the week and there wouldn't be time to design and make one at such short notice. Then she asked how much I wanted for the one I was wearing.

I detected a hint of American in the lady's accent and felt how inappropriate it was to be discussing this at the dinner table in front of other guests, but quickly – quickly – what price should I put on my first piece of jewellery. *This particular piece is three hundred pounds,* I found myself saying. It's solid silver and one of my early designs. A male voice boomed out we'll take it. It was the gentleman purporting to be her husband. I was pretty speechless. *Three hundred quid – how many days at the Sugar 'n' Spice and nights at The Garrick would I have to work to make money like that?* I thought to myself. "Great, I'll give it a quick polish, wrap it nicely and let you have it tomorrow." The male voice boomed back not to bother with all that, just give it to the lady now and handed three hundred pounds to me across the dinner table.

Three hundred pounds was a fortune. How on earth I

pulled it off, I have no idea. Wealthy Americans, two bottles of wine down the hatch, who cares? I got my first big sale, and I was thrilled. This episode was to stand me in good stead, as it gave me confidence to steer myself into the future as a goldsmith-jeweller. When I told Bryan about the sale he was delighted. Dear Bryan, with his soft sensuous voice and shock of black Romany hair sweeping over one eye, his gentle but firm manner made him a charming and irresistible young man whom I admired a lot. He had guided me well to get to this point. Bryan on the other hand was quite philosophical telling me it was a one-off, and to well remember the winter months ahead to get through in Cornwall. And if I really wanted to succeed in becoming a goldsmith, then I needed to go to London, apply for a gold licence and buy my own metals from Johnson Matthey, and apprentice myself to a workshop in Hatton Garden. Go and talk to the director of Goldsmith's Hall, do whatever it takes.

Good friends from Manchester, John and Bill, descended on St Ives, not only to see me, but to have a look around for any prospective businesses that might be on the market. They were determined to leave the north of England and move to Cornwall, for better weather, change of direction, and new beginnings. They loved the atmosphere of the small town and like most people, with four fine beaches and the Atlantic on your doorstep, what was not to like? Bill had worked in the family firm of printing and I think he wanted to have his own business and prove to his family that he could make a go of something on his own. Bill was fairly serious and straight-laced, while John could be more fun and flamboyant.

St Ives was still in the advent of the Flower Power era, which slogan is used as a symbol of passive resistance and non-violent ideology. It was rooted in the opposition movement to the Vietnam War. And we all revelled in it. Everyone seemed cheerful and happy with flowers in their hair and light-hearted flippancy abounded. It was fun; it was harmless, when the biggest crime was to steal a fresh bottle of milk from the doorstep of a Fish Street cottage early in the morning on the way home from a party. There was hash and no doubt other drugs around, but this never touched or affected me. It was there if you wanted, there if you didn't. We partied to Jim Morrison and the Doors, Bob Dylan, Joan Baez, sympathised with Leonard Cohen and danced the night away with The Beatles and surfed to the Beach Boys. The sixties at its zenith in St Ives was pure magic. But how would John and Bill fit in, this wasn't really their scene – but there again it wasn't mine either, but I loved it nonetheless.

There wasn't much time to see John and Bill but we did manage a couple of drinks at the Sloop, and a meal at The Outrigger, but there was no time to show them the sights, and from all accounts they hadn't needed me to show them anything – they'd done that all by themselves. They came to Trewyn one afternoon to tell me excitedly that they were going through the process of buying a newspaper shop in Tregenna Place – both boys were absolutely thrilled. It would need to be brought up to scratch and worked at to make it viable for both of them to get an income out of it. I had no doubt that these two young guns would make a go of it. It would be a couple of months before the transfer went through, and in the meantime they were returning to Manchester to work their butts off. Truly thrilled and really delighted that two friends would be living and working near me in St Ives, I gave them both a big hug and sent them on their way.

Other shenanigans were happening in St Ives with surfer, Colin Pryor, sending shockwaves through the town. Colin owned a shoe shop in the High Street, opposite the entrance to Will's Lane, which everyone supported as Colin was a friend. In my opinion, it was a brave attempt to open a shoe shop in St Ives, during a time when shops were opening and closing all the time, due, I presume, to high rentals and the start of cheap package holidays to Spain, France, Portugal and the Greek Islands, as well as other places on the continent that were fast becoming the rage. It was cheaper to fly to Spain than a train fare to Cornwall, with guaranteed weather, warmth and sunshine. Tourists were no longer coming to St Ives in their droves as they used to do. The package tours will soon fizzle out, everyone moaned; as yet another shop closed its doors. So it happened with Colin's shop, one day it was open and the next day it was completely empty and shut up – not a shoe in sight. Curiouser and curiouser, there was no sign of Colin either, which set alarm bells ringing.

Colin arrived in St Ives from Swindon in 1964. He had worked at a Nuclear Research place in Wiltshire; he was a good footballer who had trials with professional teams. Down here in St Ives, he was on the dole – where he got something like two thirds of his salary while looking for work in his previous field. Not a lot of need for Nuclear Researchers in Cornwall, so he was free to spend his life surfing at Porthmeor, chatting up the girls and spend most evenings in the Castle Inn with the rest of the surfers. He married Michelle, a very quiet, attractive dark-haired lady with whom he had a son. But the marriage didn't last and they eventually split up.

After the shop closed down, it was discovered that Colin had teamed up with a guy known as JD, and set themselves up as Estate Agents, which turned out to be a complete scam. These two applied for mortgages for fictitious people, scooped a load of money and went off to Ibiza, leaving everyone who knew him . . . in shock. We're hearing through the grapevine that Colin was setting up a successful sports centre there – tennis courts etcetera, and was living the 'dream lifestyle'. Carol Jackson can't forget him, as Colin made her 2nd in a Miss Porthmeor Pageant where he had the deciding vote and chose the girl he was going out with as, 1st Miss Porthmeor.

Judy, who was still annoyed with me, moved into a flat at Anchor House, and it was lovely. Norman Stocker had the ground-floor flat there, so it was inevitable that I might bump into Judy quite a lot of the time when I visited Norman, and it was only fifty yards away from Trewyn, where I was now living. She started having a relationship with one of St Ives' prominent female artists, but from what I was hearing, this relationship was not going well and there were dramas galore at Anchor House. The artist in question, of course, blamed all this on me. It was obviously a one-sided relationship as Judy did not feel the same about her new friend, as the artist felt about her. So I got the blame for being the catalyst in all of this. Interesting when you have to blame someone else because the person you're attracted to is not attracted to you. We were all young and nobody wanted 'serious' relationships. It was a life lived for each day.

Through John and Boots, I got to know some of the artists, sculptors and potters more intimately. Bryan Wynter was a good friend of Boots. They shared a great love of art and particularly abstract paintings. I could see why Boots wanted the New Craftsman to become a top art gallery – where ceramics and jewellery would become part of its collection. Bryan's paintings for a new exhibition would look pretty outstanding on the stark white-walls of the super new gallery. Of course, there would be pottery by Bernard Leach, he was after all, the country's leading potter and the husband of Janet Leach, a partner in the New Craftsman – that would perhaps bring Bernard's friend, the Japanese potter, Hamada Shoji, to show his fine work at the gallery. Another very good friend of Bernard and Janet Leach was the modern ceramic artist Lucie Rie, one of the 20th century's most celebrated and iconic potters.

Lucie Rie, together with Janet Leach and Barbara Hepworth were invited by John to dinner one evening at Trewyn. The reclusive composer, Priaulx Rainier, was also invited but declined the invitation. It was a beautiful evening, sitting having drinks in the elegant lounge with these three celebrated ladies. Lucy Rie was small and delicate with a graceful presence – she was a true lady in every sense of the word. She lived in London but was very much part of the St Ives pottery and ceramic group. Ivaldo produced a supreme dinner and managed to keep his histrionics at bay and take on his finer, prima donna role – he enchanted the ladies and, of course, they all loved John. At the end of the evening, I felt very privileged to have been in the company of such luminaries of the art world. Lucie Rie would also be exhibiting at the New Craftsman.

One of my favourite painters was Roger Hilton. Roger's portrayal of the naked female form illustrated to me an amazing talent in abstract art – Oi Yoi Yoi December 1963, I found fascinating – something about the liberation and freedom of the picture was refreshing, and it made me smile. I liked most of Rogers' paintings whatever the form – his abstract boats, landscapes and such like paintings as, Figure and Bird September 1963 were so diverse, nothing was predictable. One day, Boots suggested a drive out to visit Roger and his wife, Rose, who was also a painter, at their Botallack Moor home near St Just. In 1963, Roger had won the John Moores Painting Prize, in 1964 paintings by Hilton were shown in the British Pavilion at Venice Biennale, and in 1968 he was awarded a CBE.

We were royally received as Boots knew the Hiltons well. And I luxuriated in the very ambience of the home of these two amazing artists, painters, characters whatever – enjoying a scratched lunch thrown together haphazardly, but with great enthusiasm. It was no secret in the St Ives art community that Roger drank a lot; in fact, he drank a great deal and was an alcoholic. Sitting there at the Botallack Hilton, surrounded by the wild beauty of the West Penwith landscape and the Cornish coastline, I wondered what made someone like Roger Hilton, the talented pioneer of abstract art in post-Second World War, drink himself to the point of destruction? The trip was an experience and we enjoyed seeing Roger and Rose at their home, and discussing art, artists, galleries, and what was happening in the rest of England.

It was early evening by the time we left the Hiltons, so I suggested that we go and have an early dinner in the

Tin Mine Tavern at Trewellard near Pendeen. This was a trip down memory lane from a couple of years previously, when Keith Hall and his friend, Mike Carr, both from Penzance, took Jackie van Gelder and myself out for dinner to the Tin Mine Tavern circa 1962 – driving us from St Ives in their respective sports cars along the coast road to Pendeen. We'd met the two young men at the Life Boat Inn one evening as Jackie knew Mike, and they asked us out. Keith was a big, burly Cornishman who looked much too big for the small sports car seat that he was sitting in. Speeding along to Pendeen was exhilarating but talk was difficult due to some of the sharp bends on the road and I didn't want conversation to distract Keith.

The Tin Mine Tavern was a licensed restaurant and a veritable museum. The ceiling was supported by mine timbers. There was also a back room which has stained glass windows depicting Cornish mining scenes. There was a range of books for reading, and mineral specimens – it was full of atmosphere, lovely food and it had a good vibe, that the four of us thoroughly enjoyed. A couple of weeks later Keith and I went there again, but this time alone. Still enjoyable but not the same spark as when the four of us had been there together. No spark either in the courtship between Keith and I, other than his nice new car – and that was the end of that. I never saw him again, but I did hear about him through the Penzance grapevine now and again, as he was becoming a well-known businessman in the town.

Now I am sitting in the Tin Mine Tavern once again with Boots Redgrave. The décor, food and the atmosphere has subtlety changed since I was last there – not quite as energetic, as if being out on a limb from both St Ives and Penzance has taken its toll, the Trewellard and Pendeen locals don't earn the sort of money to be able to eat out very often, as the tin mines were closing down around them one by one. The Tin Mine Tavern building itself had once been a workshop, a fish and chip shop, a private dwelling, a café, and a hairdressing salon. With a sinking heart, I hoped this wasn't the slow slippery slide of the Tin Mine Tavern that I felt a strange attraction to. Boots liked it and we enjoyed a really nice dinner chatting to the owner, Bill, who was clearly a tin mining enthusiast. We drove back to Nancledra, having had a really eventful and happy day.

Tony O'Malley often stayed at Heather Cottage with Boots, particularly over the weekends. He once had a studio at Trevaylor before Nancy sold the house and went off to live with Conor, in Ireland. Tony himself is an Irish artist, born in Callan, County Kilkenny. He is a self-taught artist, having drawn and painted for pleasure from childhood. Tony worked as a bank clerk in Ireland, and later retired from the bank due to ill health in 1958, he began painting full-time from then. He visited St Ives in 1955 and returned to settle here in 1960. Tony has a studio just off Back Road West, where he also lives.

Due to the ongoing ill-health, and being a great friend, Boots liked to have Tony for the weekends to simply nurture him with good food, a bath, a bed and some homely company. Tony of course, thrived on it and nearly always appeared if an invitation was offered. Both Boots and I realised after a few weekends spent at Heather Cottage that Tony kept favouring a sore big toe and now appeared with a hole cut out of his shoe to accommodate the sore toe. He asked Boots if he could bathe his toe in warm water and put on some gentian violet that someone had given to him, or iodine if we had any. I leapt into action as this did not sound good. Whatever was wrong with Tony's big toe had obviously got worse instead of better, and my immediate thought leapt to gangrene. I managed to get him to remove his shoe and an excuse for a sock to reveal the putrefying toe that did not look good at all. Boots handed Tony a glass of whisky and told him to drink it while we dealt with bathing the toe.

In no uncertain terms, Boots told Tony he was going to her doctor in Penzance on Monday, she would phone for an urgent appointment, and asked me if I would take him.

Of course, I'd take him, I told her, and Tony stayed cossetted at Heather Cottage for the rest of the weekend. True to her word, on Monday morning, Boots had phoned her doctor in Penzance and an appointment was made for 11 a.m. Tony and I always got on well and made each other laugh – I loved his Irish brogue, the wicked twinkle in his eye and his naughtiness. As a painter, he was getting better all the time and beginning to exhibit at more galleries. Boots had great faith in Tony's work, and felt that one day he would aspire to become a great artist.

Dr Slack saw Tony and was not happy with the toe, and immediately made arrangements for him to go to the local West Cornwall Hospital in Penzance to have a biopsy taken from his toe – so off we went. When Tony came out of seeing the specialist and having the biopsy done, he was visibly shaken and insisted he needed a drink. So off we went to a nearby pub where he downed a couple of Irish Whiskies – apparently the biopsy experience had not been a pleasant one. I decided to take Tony back to Heather Cottage, instead of taking him to his studio in St Ives – it felt the right thing to do to keep an eye on him until he got over the hospital visit.

Two weeks later, we returned to the Hospital to see the specialist about the results of Tony's toe biopsy. If I thought he looked shaken from the biopsy, hearing the results of it had shocked him to the core. "It's cancer," he told me as I went to greet him, "cancer, can you believe it?" Tony suddenly looked twenty years older, bewildered and visibly shaking. The prognosis being that the toe needed to be amputated as soon as possible before the cancer spread into his foot. The specialist was making arrangements as we talked. Tony would be admitted to the hospital two days later. We drove back to Heather Cottage in silence, as I couldn't come up with anything to say to break the tension or cheer Tony up.

Everything happened very quickly after that. Boots took Tony when he was admitted to the hospital for his operation. She served as his next-of-kin as he didn't have anyone else, and he trusted Boots with his life. A few days after the operation, Tony was allowed home and Boots went to collect him. The amputation had gone well and the doctors were confident that it hadn't spread further than his big toe – he had a walking stick and would have physiotherapy to help him to walk properly again. The big toe (the hallux), helps your walk and balance – losing the toe means you have to learn to adjust your walk and balance without it. Tony's pain improved a week after surgery and the stitches were removed after ten days. Already he looked like a different man – the cancer had not spread and given a few weeks, he would be as right as rain and walking perfectly, provided he looked after the wound and looked after himself. We would be helping him on both counts.

Beloved Tony made a remarkable recovery and we were all proud of him and the way in which he handled the situation. He walked better, looked better and even painted better – so the entire 'Big Toe' conundrum was soon forgotten as life took on a new meaning. A group of artists and friends living and working around Tony kept an eye on him. It wasn't long before we began to hear fluttering's of a young lady in Tony's life – her name was Jane, from Montreal in Canada, an artist and thirty-one years his junior. It seemed too good to be true. When Tony brought Jane to Heather Cottage one weekend to meet Boots and I, we were enchanted with the lovely blonde-haired, gentle Jane who clearly adored Tony as he adored her. Long may it last, we both rejoiced, waving them off on Sunday afternoon.

Chapter Eight

Trewyn

Living at Trewyn most of the time as well as working there brought its advantages and its disadvantages. First and foremost, the owner of Trewyn, John Milne, was an artist and a sculptor. The guest house side of Trewyn was merely a guise, set up for John's many well-known and influential friends from London and around the world. John was a perfectionist, the guest house was run to perfection, the food was superb, and John himself always looked immaculate in whatever he wore. His taste in classical music was second to none, and throwing all this together into Trewyn made it the success that it was. But up and above all this, John craved to be a successful sculptor, to have the recognition like his famous friend and neighbour, Barbara Hepworth.

Born in Eccles, Lancashire on 23rd June 1931, he studied electrical engineering at Salford Royal Technical College 1945, then transferred to the Art School at the Technical College, specialising in sculpture until 1951. Studied at Académie de la Grande Chaumiere, Paris 1952. Then became a pupil and later assistant to Barbara Hepworth in 1952 – 4. John bought Trewyn (with the help of his friend, Professor Cosmo Rodewald), a beautiful house with a garden adjoining Hepworth's studio in 1957.

One of the great advantages for me living at Trewyn was being amongst fine works of art, pottery, and sculpture. John didn't necessarily like anyone being in his studio when he was working – but he didn't mind me popping in with a mug of coffee or tea, then he would allow me to stay and watch for a while. I remember when the sculpture 'Gnathos' arrived back from the foundry, we were all excited, and once John had done the finishing touches to it and polished the bronze and the black

Belgium marble base of fingerprints, it looked truly impressive. John's charcoal drawings to me were something special. He was certainly a gifted artist – he had some of his framed drawings hung in the interior at Trewyn, showing them off on the large walls, together with a sculpture or two on plinths in the hallway and on the stairs – a couple of bronzes stood outside on the terrace. It was an art gallery in itself.

Apart from Barbara Hepworth, John had another fellow sculptor friend in St Ives, Denis Mitchell. At one point, both John and Denis worked together for Barbara, at her Trewyn Studio. I met Denis several times through John and liked him a lot. Hard to imagine this robustly charming man was a market gardener, a tin miner at Geevor and a fisherman before becoming a sculptor. He was a founder member of the Penwith Society in 1949-59 and the Chairman of the Penwith Society from 1955-7. His works in bronze 'Turning Form' and in Nigerian guarea wood (the wood bought from Barbara Hepworth) 'Oracle', are amongst my favourites.

An admirable lady called Marjorie Parr arrived at Trewyn to stay for a few days. She was a guest of John's. Marjorie owned an art gallery in London, which she'd previously run as an antique shop. At first, she began to show modern art in the basement – then the whole building was used for showing art including work by St Ives artists. This is where John met Marjorie, and the two became instant friends. I think that Marjorie mothered John a lot, which he seemed to enjoy, and it was good to see him laughing and happy when she was around.

This was to prove a fruitful visit for Marjorie and St Ives artists as she ended up enthusiastically, buying a property in Wills Lane, a two-minute walk from Trewyn and the Marjorie Parr, Wills Lane Gallery was born. It would be some while before the property was transferred and re-furbished to Marjorie's taste – and she would have to spend quite a bit of time in St Ives overlooking the change. There's a lovely flat attached to Trewyn with a private entrance accessed in Ayr Lane. The flat belonged to John's friend and benefactor, Cosmo Rodewald, to use for his visits to St Ives. Like the rest of the house, the flat was nicely furnished, and John allowed only special people to use it (in consultation with Cosmo), so he offered the flat to Marjorie to use while she overlooked the work on the Wills Lane property. Once the gallery was up and running, Marjorie would live in the small flat above it.

It was a special time when the Marjorie Parr – Wills Lane Gallery opened its doors. The gallery itself was small in comparison to a lot of the galleries that were springing up left, right, and centre. Marjorie somehow had a knack for choosing the right artists, sculptors and potters for her gallery – and what's more, she sold them. The good and the great of the famous Cornish art colony exhibited at the Wills Lane Gallery such as Wilhelmina Barnes-Graham, Denis Mitchell, John Milne, Patrick Heron, John Wells, Bernard Leach, Janet Leach, and Barbara Hepworth to name but a few. It was a hugely profitable gallery; Marjorie was successful and managed it beautifully. The tall, thin, amusing and unassuming Marjorie Parr – circa early sixties, was a hit in St Ives.

Of course, this didn't please a lot of the lesser-known painters, potters, and sculptors because they weren't chosen to exhibit at the new Wills Lane Gallery; it would appear that only the leading lights of the art colony got to exhibit their work there. This wasn't exactly true, as Marjorie did show work from lesser-known artists during the Gallery's first two years. Knowing Marjorie quite well by this time, I would imagine to keep the gallery open and running she did need to have the more saleable work of established artists to prop up the incoming, lesser-known artists. She was as cool as a cucumber when it came to business was Marjorie, and in my opinion, she had a superb eye and instinct for seeking out new work by less well-known, painters and craftsmen.

The disadvantage of living at Trewyn was not having my own room and privacy. I slept at the top of the house between John's bedroom and Ivaldo's bedroom in an in-between room that was more probably a dressing room. Out of season, I could use one of the guest rooms. It was fun to start off with – all three of us being hunkered up at the top of the house. John's large studio bedroom had long glass sliding doors leading onto a balcony that had a fabulous view over the harbour and the ocean beyond.

Unfortunately, John had to pass through my room to get to his room, and if he'd had a row with Ivaldo – as the relationship was becoming strained – I was in the middle of it. The fiery, impetuous Italian in a foul mood was not a pleasant sight. Ivaldo's room was on the other side of the stairway leading up to our rooms, it was small, shut away and private. I think John felt safer with Ivaldo on the other side of the stairway – but that didn't help me. So I found myself spending more time at Heather Cottage. In fact, Boots had suggested that I turn a small unused space into a jewellery workroom – and I did.

So, when I was off-duty at Trewyn, the chances were I'd be honing my jewellery skills at Heather Cottage or with Bryan and Breon at their workshop. These were special times, and I learned such a lot from watching these two goldsmiths creating their pieces. Breon O'Casey is the son of Irish nationalist and playwright, Sean O'Casey. Breon is a big man with a large black beard and dark-brown Irish eyes, whose persona looks more like that of a miner than the delicate craft of goldsmithing. He is a quiet and peaceful man with a hidden sense of humour. Married to Doreen, they have two daughters and one son. I never saw the O'Casey's at any social events in St Ives, I suspect they were a close unit, happy within their family life.

Travelling through to Heather Cottage fairly frequently, on occasions I would call in to see the painter, Victor Bramley, and his wife Jacque, who lived in a row of cottages as you entered the village of Nancledra. This is where Victor first worked on his paintings before renting the village mill that was empty and commandeered that as a studio. Victor ran away from an industrial background in

Sheffield where his family were butchers and set off in the direction of Cornwall. He started out in St Ives washing dishes, but within two years he was elected a member of the St Ives Society of Artists, after being discovered by the society who spotted his work in the Craftsman shop in Fore Street, where Victor and Jacque were working at the time.

Victor's work was interesting; he loved to paint boats, the sea, elements of the countryside, boulders, rocks, and pebbles in strong forms. He was equally at home in a variety of styles and genres. He married Jacque Moran, the sister of my friend, Phil Moran, in 1960. Jacque was quite a corker of a girl, good-looking and loved by everyone in St Ives. She was the one-time, great love of infamous artist, sculptor, and writer, Sven Berlin. It was always good to catch up with these two friends, enjoy a coffee and chat about life in St Ives and get news of Captain Phil, who is a Master Mariner and always away at sea.

I also like to call in and see Alan Lowndes, who lives in Halsetown, which is on the way to Nancledra. Another northerner like me, John Milne, and Victor Bramley, Alan was born in Heaton Norris, Lancashire, a suburb of Stockport. He is known primarily for his scenes of northern life and is a close friend of many of the St Ives school of artists. In the 1950's, he shared a studio with Michael Broido, and then had the Piazza Studio of Linden Travers (the sister of Bill Travers of Born Free fame). Later, he painted in a sail loft in Norway Square and then in one of the Porthmeor Studios, before moving to Halsetown in 1964.

Apart from his paintings of northern life, he was passionate about Porthmeor Beach which he painted and sketched. Alan's depiction of St Ives 'Harbour in Autumn', 'The Intrepid Paddlers', 'Beach Scene' and 'Sea Meets Sky', are amongst some of the most interesting non-abstract paintings around, well, I certainly think so. He had a studio built in the garden at Halsetown, and this is where we often sat and talked about art, his friends down in the town, his wife, and family. For a short time in the flower picking season, I had rented a cottage in Halsetown and loved it. It was nice people like the Lowndes, Keith and Mary Barron, who made this little enclave such a special place.

The Cortina Café at the top of The Warren became another favourite meeting place, as well as The Blue Haven, further down The Warren, for the local art colony. Being able to sit outside at the Cortina was a plus in my case, so dependent on weather, I would arrange to meet up with one or other of my friends who were fast becoming ignored due to me working at Trewyn all hours, and trying to improve my skills as a jeweller. It was good to catch up with Greta, Carol, Robin, and Norman whenever possible. Peggy Frank, my landlady at the Academy Steps flat, owned or rented a shop-cum gallery on a corner of Back Road West – I often saw Bob Bourne hanging around in there either painting or looking after the gallery.

I don't think Bob being in there did the place any favours as he always looked dirty, scruffy and down-at-heel, being tall, long-haired, and gaunt with an unpleasant whiff, he truly was the epitome of the penniless artist. Peggy was forever moaning about him whenever we met up, either in the gallery or at her home, Academy House, if I'd dropped in for coffee.

Carol and I were passing Peggy's gallery one afternoon after a swim on Porthmeor, and there as large as life in situ was Bob Bourne. Bob left as we entered, and Peggy suddenly set forth complaining about him always hanging around. Carol and I looked at each other in exasperation and then asked Peggy why on earth she put up with him or allowed him to be there at all. "Well, he does look awful and smells a bit, but he's very good in bed," she announced. I don't know if it was the shock of Peggy saying this or the sheer fact that someone could possibly go near Bob, let alone have sex with him. Well, there's no accounting for taste, we agreed, after leaving the gallery, and the impossible Mrs Frank.

Arthur Caddick and his wife, Peggy live in a cottage aptly named, Windswept, above the village of Nancledra. Another northerner from Yorkshire who, after working at the War Office during the Second World War, moved his family to Cornwall in 1945. Sven Berlin and his family also lived on the outskirts of Nancledra. The Caddick and the Berlin families were, for many years, good friends. Their children played together, the parents socialised on a regular basis. Peggy Caddick was like an aunt to the Berlin youngsters.

In the end it all went sour, culminating in Sven Berlin's publication of 'The Dark Monarch' in 1962 – several years after he had left St Ives. The allegedly defamatory content caused Arthur Caddick and others to bring a libel action which, although it never came to court, they effectively won. In their day, Arthur tells me, he and Sven Berlin were the two most colourful and talented of the fabled artistic community, and I believed him. Arthur is a talented poet, who has written several books of poetry, including Tales for Children, illustrated by artist, Alan Lowndes and his autobiography, Laughter from Land's End and his much loved poem, Cuckoo-Song:

> *O Auntie! Fetch the family tree!*
> *Have I Cornish blood in me?*
> *Did my forebears ever rove*
> *Somewhere round by Lanyon Cove?*
> *Did they chase the fairies in*
> *The mystic darkness of the glynn?*
> *Did they live on Bodmin's hills!*
> *Roasting goats for Celtic grylls?*
> *O Auntie! Fetch our pedigree!*
> *Have I Cornish blood in me?*
> *If I'm not a proper Celt,*
> *Do I hit below the belt*
> *If I say that now and then,*
> *I've seen the little whimsey men,*

Leaping on the Bottrall Downs,
Laughing like demented clowns?
The cuckoo calls! I must, I must
Become a Cornishman or bust.
Buy up scores of family trees,
Bottrallize me, Auntie please!
And then – O then! – no cuckoo, I
Shall sing canary-like on high,
Fed on proper Celtic groundsel
From the Ancient British Council.

Polarthur Trebruce Pencaddick

Reading this poem always amuses me and I often wonder if Sven Berlin depicted St Ives as Cuckoo in his book 'The Dark Monarch', after Arthur Caddick uses Cuckoo for not being a Cornishman, in the poem. I'm guessing that Cuckoo – Song circa 1955, was written before Sven wrote his controversial, fictionalised autobiography that was published in 1962, and withdrawn a few days later. It somehow didn't feel right asking Arthur about this. Life can't have been easy for the Caddick's out at Nancledra, but they were a tight knit-family and seemed content with their lot. Arthur would joke and bang on about visiting St Ives as a special occasion, going to the cinema and Woolworth's was an outing – and always snappily dressed wearing his legendary . . . haphazard bowtie. His poem The Homestead, sums the Caddick's life up for me . . . the last four lines:

We stand together with the children playing,
This is a day when happiness goes deep.
Hold tight my hand! Let's run and join their laughter
There will be nights when one of us must weep.

Arthur Caddick 1955

Described as the poet laureate of Cornwall, Arthur Caddick wrote some wonderful poetry about publicans, bohemians, the Cornish countryside and his St Ives art colony friends, some becoming famous before him, such as Bryan Wynter, Peter Lanyon, Alan Lowndes; even Bernard Leach casually dropped into the tiny Windswept cottage, where the family lived a life so frugal, it is scarcely credible.

On cold, windy days I loved to walk around the Island from Porthgwidden watching the Atlantic waves throw themselves up against the rocks below, the power of the sea always amazing me. Then across Porthmeor on to Clodgy Point, the bracing, salty spume slashing across my face burrowing deep into my long tendrilled hair. Refreshing, but ultimately cleansing. I make my way back to another favourite spot, the fishermen's lodges, Rose and Shamrock on Wharf Road or, Shore Shelter, opposite the Sloop Inn, where I needed a warm, dry place to go and be amongst my fisherman friends. Sir Edward Hain funded the lodges to be built for the fishermen of St Ives many, many years ago as a warm, dry place to go whenever they needed to be near their boats. Whether it be waiting for the tide or keeping an eye on the boats in the harbour in stormy conditions. Or just to meet fellow-fishermen for a chat.

Whenever I go in, it's like stepping back in time – you can still feel the presence of the old boys that have long gone. There are still quite a few of the St Ives elders left that no longer go to sea, which is great to be able to sit and listen to their tales. It's a wonderful part of St Ives that I believe must be preserved. The insides are adorned with old photographs of past fishing boats, catches, wrecks and events. Today, I will pop into Shore Shelter and sit for a while to get warm and dry, listening to the chatter of the fishermen – some of whom I'd been introduced to in the bar of the Sloop by my fisherman boyfriend, Seth – enjoying time with these seafaring men, was the best.

There's been a great brouhaha circulating around the town that Bernard Leach (CBE 1962) Dame Barbara Hepworth (appointed DBE 1965) and Ben Nicholson (OM 1968) are to be given Honorary Freedom of the Borough of St Ives, in recognition of their International Contribution to the Arts, in a ceremony to be held at the Guildhall in Street-an-Pol. This news has set the art colony and St Ives in general, a-buzzing. Instead of feeling proud that three of the local artists and residents are having this great honour bestowed upon them, it would appear that there are a hundred-odd other persons more deserving of this honour. Such is nature in a small community, no matter how much we talked about it, nobody really wanted to acknowledge this honour. Bernard, Barbara and Ben already have a CBE, a DBE, and an OM respectively, stowed upon them by the Queen, why do they need more, the ill-informed gossips bleated?

On and on it went until the natural course of events took over and the entire episode lost its momentum, as Barbara Hepworth, followed by Bernard Leach and his wife Janet, came proudly down the steps of The Guildhall, as Honourably Appointed Freedom of the Borough of St Ives recipients. Together with Ben Nicholson, I thought it was well-deserving as these iconic St Ives artists have been pioneers of their trade long before the present generation of artists came along – putting St Ives very clearly. . . on the map.

John allowed me to keep the Frogeye Sprite in the garage at Trewyn, which was a huge bonus as the parking in St Ives during the summer months is impossible. There was another car, a Mercedes Benz convertible permanently parked in the garage that belonged to Cosmo, for the odd times he and his friend, Victor visited St Ives, staying in the flat at Trewyn. John liked nothing more than going on occasional outings during the day, one of his favourites being Helford Creek, where there were a couple of small restaurants that he liked to go to. To have lunch sitting out on the little terraces overlooking the river immortalised in

Daphne Du Maurier's book, Frenchman's Creek.

Today, we're going to Helford and John's asking me if I would drive us there in the Mercedes – of course, I accepted as this was a great opportunity for me to drive this beautiful sports car. Unfortunately, the garage was as far as I got. Sitting in the Mercedes it felt enormous, everything about it was large and overpowering. It also had automatic transmission and being a dedicated, four-gears girl, I really didn't have the courage to manoeuvre it out of the garage, let alone drive it through the narrow streets and bends of St Ives. John was disappointed as we bundled ourselves into the Sprite and made our way to Helford.

I told him he should learn to drive himself if he wanted to use the Mercedes. Both John and I loved the Roseland Peninsula, St Just in Roseland and St Mawes, which we sometimes visited. Today, we are driving through the old port of Gweek, at the head of the Helford River on towards Manaccan, then Helford Creek. Parking the car in a field on the outskirts of the village – we walked down the hill past the well-known, Riverside Restaurant, around the head of the creek to the other side of the river. We admired the quaint cottages and gardens as we went, eventually finding our destination, Rose Cottage, one of the prettiest little lunchtime restaurants in the area, which serves fresh salmon, oysters, prawns, and crab. Light lunches, perfectly presented, surrounded by an abundance of rose bushes and a view across the river – life couldn't be better.

As an artist, John was gaining momentum, especially since Marjorie Parr came onto the scene. Our house guest list consisted of such interesting people as Patricia Neal, wife of Roald Dahl, followed by film director, John Schlesinger arriving with a host of starlets, and other filmmakers from America, turning Trewyn into a kind of Starlight Hotel. But it was great, as people arrived and left, leaving us all breathless in their wake. Some of these wealthy people bought a John Milne sculpture here and there, costing an amount of money that made my eyes water. On the other hand, I was also selling quite a few pieces of my own jewellery to these eminent guests, which boosted my morale until I believed that I was fast becoming a goldsmith . . . London was calling.

A new pub on the block, The Lifeboat Inn, on Wharf Road just a few doors away from St Ives lifeboat station, has at last opened its doors, so for a couple of weeks, it became the popular place to have a drink, meet friends and influence people. After dinner at Trewyn, guests and ourselves would go for a nightcap at this newly-opened establishment – it was always crowded and difficult to get to the bar and therefore to get drinks, making the evening late and everyone irritable. In these cases, we made our way back to Trewyn via the Castle Inn, where usually, a welcome awaited us in the back bar by the landlords, Stan and Stella Jackson.

But of late, our very own Ivaldo Ferrari, of fine cuisine fame at Trewyn, has suddenly decided to spread his skills and is now – as well as head chef at Trewyn – a barman at the Castle, running his own one-man show, being as bossy with customers as he was with everyone else. But Stan and Stella were very fond of him, and so indeed, were the customers – a true prima donna of the highest order, boosting the Castle Inn's food and liquor sales beyond expectations. He turns his nose up when he sees we've arrived at the Castle just before closing time, having not managed too well getting drinks at the Lifeboat and shuffles off to the front bar to get one of the less important bar staff to serve us.

Guest dinners were only served three evenings a week (bookings only) at Trewyn. Recently, Ivaldo has suddenly taken it upon himself to ask my friend, Robin, – also a chef, to help him out in the kitchen with the breakfasts and occasionally in the evening when more than eight or ten guests had booked dinner. Robin proved very helpful, so Ivaldo took advantage of this and had taken the part-time job at the Castle, which, in a way, was a relief for all of us not having his vitriolic temperament to deal with, and the constant bickering between himself and John to put up with. I loved Ivaldo, and all the guests adored him, he was a showman. But at this time, his relationship with John, who he loved and cared about, was not reciprocated any longer, causing massive tension between the two, and therefore throughout the house, particularly when guests were not around. Even the much loved cats, Puccio and Ting took cover at these times. His snubbing us at the Castle was all part of his act, mainly to draw attention to himself. He soon came round to the back bar because he couldn't bear to miss out on anything.

I am not really a pub person and wouldn't go into one unless with a friend or in a group. My forays into the Lifeboat Inn and the Castle Inn were merely at the invitation of John or some of the guests having dinner at Trewyn, where a group of four, six or eight, to them, seemed to be more fun. Sometimes, I joined them, and sometimes I didn't, depending on who the guests were. My idea of a pub can only be the Sloop Inn. And to add to that, it can only be the front bar. This, to me, is like walking into my own world with its low, smoke-stained, low beamed ceiling. The walls were festooned with photographs and caricatures of fishermen, some still here and some long gone, of framed Giles cartoons, paintings, and drawings by artists in lieu of payment. There is a small window and window seat in the corner, the two long bar tables (one holding the bar skittles) and benches and two or three bar stools with an ancient settle seat at the end, filled the room.

But, of course, it was the group of fishermen bunched around the far end of the bar, some as steeped in character as the Sloop itself puffing on their well-worn pipes, with other middle-aged and younger fishermen around them, with an artist or two on the periphery. But all banded together in the moaning and groaning of hail-hearted poverty. These were the people I enjoyed so much and loved spending time with. Known now as, Seth's girl

– I'd been accepted by these fishermen as they never encouraged or talked to any of the tourists or anyone else for that matter if they could help it. Theirs was a tight-knit community, local-born and bred, men of the sea always, slowly but surely being shoehorned out of their boats, pilchard cellars, sail-lofts, and homes by the onslaught of artists and tourism descending on St Ives. And with the fishing industry on the decline, the fate of the town's fishermen was being sealed.

I'm getting news from Jack Richards, who owns Old Quay House, Griggs Quay on the mouth of the Hayle estuary where Betty and Liz are still living. It's good news because her London friend, Jane Relf, has mentioned to a singer-songwriter connected with The Yardbirds, Jim McCarty, that her friend in Cornwall is a poet and songwriter. He's sent Betty some music for her to write the words to. When I eventually manage to get over to see Betty, she tells me that a couple of her songs have been accepted by the new group, Renaissance. The Yardbirds disbanded as Keith Relf, and drummer, Jim McCarty, wanted to explore a new sound blending elements of rock, folk and classical music together and formed Renaissance. Betty is totally nonchalant about this debut into the world of rock bands, saying she found it easy and perfectly natural to write the words. This must have been a great breakthrough, knowing her talent was being recognised and paying off.

Betty told me through our various conversations when first we'd met that she was born in Paddington in 1944, and her name was Betty Mary Newsinger. She had been a gifted child who read newspapers at home and won a scholarship to the local grammar school after passing her 11-plus. However, she already displayed some of the chronic shyness that made her write under the name Thatcher to preserve her anonymity (her mother married in 1949 in Hammersmith, London, and became Mrs Thatcher). Her reluctance to sit further exams stalled her academic progress until she moved to another school, where her talent for the arts and her way with the English language were allowed to blossom. I was glad to hear in her own words that she was now concentrating on the art of writing. Being a natural scribe and doodler, there were notes and scraps of paper a-plenty, but that was all that there appeared to be. Nothing of substance turned up in writing form. Well, maybe that was the way in which Betty wrote. After all, she was not about to shut herself away and write a tome.

For her, life was pretty good with a new friend, a settled home in which to live, and a smattering of like-minded people to whom she could discuss and sort out the world's problems. Being a campaigner for Nuclear Disarmament (CND), hating the apartheid Government and rallying freedom for Nelson Mandela in South Africa, gave vent for her frustration. Telling me the haunting songs of Leonard Cohen, Bob Dylan, and Joan Baez, ringing around St Ives and Hayle in a circumnavigation of meetings, the odd party, silent séances, and a philosophical group was putting planet earth to rights, with a few joints here and there to relax the mind and enlighten the soul.

Carol and I often went for a quick swim and sunbathe on the harbour front, by Kitty's Corner, where a nice patch of sand welcomed us. It was so refreshing after a shift of work, or in between shifts whenever time and opportunity took our fancy. We'd walk along the wharf looking for a good spot, chit-chatting away as we were wont to do. Best of all we liked to see our friend, Bob Devereaux, the man who hired out deckchairs, and stop for a chat – we were both very fond of Bob, and he seemed to enjoy us popping by. His stories fascinated us so much that we often ended up sitting on the wall where the deck chairs were piled up and listen while this talented, tall and proud librettist enchanted us with poetry that he recited there and then for everyone to hear. But, not only was Bob a librettist and a poet, he was also a painter, which begs the question – why is he a deckchair attendant?

In 1969, Bob bought a Heidelberg Printing Press

with the intention of printing poetry books and ultimately fine art prints, but things went wrong. Orders had started to come in, but despite this, the bank would no longer support the business, and Bob was left with a debt to pay off on the initial investment. To help with his finances, Bob became a deckchair attendant on St Ives Harbourfront, working from 7.30 a.m. to 6 p.m. and then working as a waiter in the evenings.

He still finds time, however, to involve himself in the organisation of cultural activities. He's just helped to organise a fringe festival for St Ives which involved 230 performers from all over the region. It brought with it some personal success for Bob because of his poetry readings which he performed with Jim Hughes, accompanying him on guitar. They were invited to tour university circuits and clubs during the winter months, performing under the name of Mask. Later, they were joined by violinist Bridget Tickner. Having put down his brush for a while, Bob has taken up painting again, while working on the deckchairs, he is ready to exhibit and is having a small exhibition of harbour paintings in watercolour at St Ives library which, I am sure, will be a virtual sell-out, as Bob is a much loved and cherished St Ives icon.

John and Bill have at last opened their newsagent shop, Watson & Jones, in Tregenna Place and are doing great trade, putting every inch of their energy into the new venture. The local people seem to love them, and the shop has absolutely everything in it from cards, stationery, newspapers, magazines, and gifts. It looks good and welcoming; therefore it's become the popular place to drop into on a daily basis. The boys have bought a cottage in a hamlet called, Towednack, about two miles out of St Ives, and it's lovely. On remote weekends off, they would invite friends for Sunday lunch and long walks in the surrounding countryside to Cripplesease or even as far as Zennor. These were heady days, full of fun and laughter, of love never gained and hearts never won, but they were our days, we were young, and we revelled in it all.

Greta has called to ask if we could meet for coffee sometime soon as she has something important to tell me. I'm gripped with something churning in my stomach as her tone sounds serious. We meet at the Cortina Café up The Warren where we're less likely to bump into anyone. Greta is already there when I arrive, looking gaunt sitting at an outside table. We greet each other, and I order a coffee as the eager waitress is standing right next to me. A sense of foreboding looms as I lower myself onto a chair opposite her. She looks at me with such a serious expression that I'm instantly thinking she's about to tell me some bad health news like she's got a life-threatening illness or something. Gearing myself up for this, I give her my undivided attention and wait. What eventually comes out is about as far from being diagnosed with a life-threatening illness as flying to the moon.

Greta tells me with all the drama and seriousness of a RADA student with the quivering lower lip that she is in love with a female potter, and wants my advice on what she should do about it. If the earth had opened up and swallowed me, I couldn't have been more stunned – at what exactly, I'm not too sure. This sudden announcement was not what I expected. Greta being attracted to a woman, was not in itself the end of the world. Being attracted to this particular potter – is what stunned me.

Composing myself, I told Greta that I was the last person to be seeking advice on relationships. I'd not had many to have gained experience, so it would be inappropriate of me to offer any to her. What I did suggest was she drop the whole thing like a red hot poker, it would go nowhere and lead to disaster. Playing a game and flattery on Janet's part, being in the bed of a famous St Ives potter on Greta's part was a recipe for disaster. This response went down like a lead balloon and knocked the ex-RADA student off her perch. She was in love, she kept insisting. "What's the problem then," I kept asking.

This was a drama Queen of quieter proportions than Ivaldo, but nonetheless, equally as dramatic. It was time for me to leave, and it couldn't come soon enough. Wild horses wouldn't have pulled Greta out of this new relationship, of that I am sure. It would find its own meteor and die its own death as naturally and organically as it was meant to be. Taking Pedn Olver steps down to Porthminster Beach where the tide was out, I walked back into the town along the shoreline, feeling refreshed and carefree.

Chapter Nine

Botallack

Being drawn to Botallack and the Crown Engine Houses of the defunct tin mines, sitting majestically but precariously on the rocks, I would grab the opportunity to go there any time anyone suggested a trip out towards Land's End and make a detour via Botallack. By this time I was fast becoming a good tour guide of that particular area and found friends, or visitors from Trewyn, so fascinated by the Engine Houses and derelict mine shafts, that we rarely made it any further. Of particular fascination was the Arsenic Labyrinth. Built in 1906, these chambers were used to collect the deadly poison, which was a by-product of the tin production process. The tin ore was heated in the large oven-like calciner to separate the tin. During this process, arsenic and sulphur fumes were given off. These were drawn through tunnels in to the arsenic labyrinth and then out of the tall chimney stack next to the complex. When operating, the chambers were closed off with iron doors, and the temperature inside would reach 600 degrees centigrade. After the chamber cooled, mineworkers would go in and scrape the powder off the walls and collect it. Safety equipment included cotton wool nose plugs, handkerchiefs for breathing through and arms smeared with clay – a teaspoon of pure arsenic can kill six men.

Botallack was a submarine mine, with tunnels extending under the sea, in places for half a mile. Over its recorded lifetime, the mine produced around 14,500 tonnes of tin, 20,000 tons of copper and 1,500 tonnes of arsenic. In 1865, the Prince and Princess of Wales visited and descended down the shaft, creating a mini-boom in tourism that caused the mine operators to charge visitors a guinea per person. The managers decided in January 1883, to stop the Botallack and Crown engines because the number of men employed below ground was not sufficient to meet the costs of keeping the engines going. The mine closed in 1895 as a result of falling tin and copper prices.

The nearby Geevor and South Crofty mines between Pendeen and Trewellard are still hanging in there. During the 20th century, Geevor drove over 85 miles of tunnels from which it produced around 50,000 tons of black tin and made a profit of over £7 million. On average, over a million gallons of water, a quarter of which was seawater, was pumped from the mine daily. Today, tin mining has taken a dive, and the call for it has slumped dramatically. I read every week now in The St Ives Times and Echo, and the Cornishman newspapers, advertisements offering tin miners in Cornwall to relocate to South Africa where tin and gold mining is still in abundance, prospering and growing, which ironically, goes almost back to the start.

At the turn of the 20th century, a group of St Just miners who had emigrated to South Africa was forced to return by the outbreak of the Second Boer War. They leased the area and conducted more thorough prospecting, being encouraged enough to set up a company called Levant North (Wheal Geevor) in 1901. From the end of World War II until the early 1960s both Geevor and South Crofty found it hard to raise capital and to recruit skilled miners. Both mines took on Polish and Italian miners. New investment, forward-looking management, and rising tin prices in the 1960s improved matters, and at this time 270 staff were employed by the mine. Now there is much underground exploration; this includes extending into the undersea workings of the Levant mine that had closed in 1930. Work is complicated by a hole in the seabed that first has to be plugged before the workings can be drained.

My heart constantly goes out to these miners whose families and history date back to the more flourishing times of tin mining. But I see and sometimes feel that the end is nigh for the mining industry, as tin prices slump by the day, and mines are closing every week throughout the

Cornish Peninsula. South Africa is offering a better deal and a better life, which in such precarious times, look attractive. Standing on the cliffs above Botallack and Geevor mines, looking out across the wild Atlantic, I thought, *if you climb down these cliffs into a boat below and sailed south, you would end up on the African continent*. I often wondered if some of the miners whose livelihoods were hanging in the balance thought the same.

I had spent so much time showing people Botallack Mine and the Arsenic Labyrinth during these past years, then The St Ives Arts Club announced they would be having a small stage production of Arsenic and Old Lace. It was to be held in the charming upstairs theatre of The Arts Club on Westcott's Quay, in the coming month. It felt appropriate to get together some friends and go to see it. The atmosphere of this little theatre would be perfect where, I believe, it is a privilege to sit watching a performance, hearing and feeling the waves crashing against the building and the sea spray coming over the roof. And, of course, the view from the window must be one of the best in St Ives. I was really looking forward to this one.

Discovery of the Ivory Cutting Works at the top of The Stennack, tucked away in what looks like some woods, on the right before the road forks off to Halsetown and the other road to Zennor, was an amazing find. It was pointed out from the top of a bus, on a ride back into St Ives by one of the passengers sitting in front of me. When he saw he'd captured my interest, the passenger, in his strong Cornish drawl, went on to tell me that they cut the ivory from large elephant tusks and made them into piano keys. Now I'm fascinated and cannot believe I've been in St Ives all this long while and never heard mention of the Ivory Works. Curiosity took me for a long walk up Higher Stennack, past the Leach Pottery and on until I eventually found a little lane that led to the Ivory Works. Not having a clue why I was actually making this visit, other than being nosey.

As I stepped inside the small factory, a bearded gentleman in his forties, looked up from a massive elephant tusk clamped in a vice-like piece of machinery that he was working on, looking completely nonplussed at my appearance. I explained to Eddie – as he'd introduced himself, that I was a jeweller and enquired if it might be possible to purchase some small pieces of ivory to incorporate in my jewellery. Quite adamantly, he said no! The ivory was not for sale to anyone off the street and didn't enlighten further on that. It was a smallish set-up, and the pungent smell of the ivory being cut and ground was overbearing, and the entire place was covered in fine white dust. I thanked Eddie and made my way to the door, when he suddenly came over and handed me a few small pieces of ivory, saying I could have these offcuts and hoped they might be useful. Feeling thrilled, I filled my pockets with the precious pieces and headed off down The Stennack, back into St Ives.

I first met Sarah Williamson, the daughter of Henry Williamson, the author of Tarka the Otter – at the Old Poor House next to Patrick Heron's house, Eagles Nest, in Zennor. A small group of artists, writers and poets had been invited for an afternoon of readings and exchanging ideas on art. Sarah, a very beautiful looking young lady with long dark hair and an open, infectious smile, is a couple of years younger than me and holds no pretention of being the daughter of such a well-known author. Sarah appeared to be living in The Poor House, most probably as a guest of Patrick Heron, but I couldn't be sure, and it was not my business to inquire. I was just delighted to have been asked – this being due perhaps to my love of writing and reading poetry.

The group included Arthur Caddick, Tony O'Malley, Hyman Segal, Bryan Wynter, and Roger Hilton. The view from the Old Poor House window stretched across the fields to the great ocean beyond, it was powerful and wild. Tregarthen Cottage sits in a row of three cottages on the track below the Poor House, leading to Tregarthen

Farm. This was once the retreat of D.H. Lawrence and his German-born wife, Frieda, who arrived in Cornwall in December 1915, and stayed for nearly two years at a rental of £5 per year. It seemed incredible to be looking down upon such a piece of history.

None of us was entirely sure why the others had been chosen for this little soirée of Sarah's, but we all milled in and found chairs and cushions to sit on. Arthur Caddick, being a well-known and voluble local character, was still preening from the aftermath of his successful libel case against Sven Berlin, where 'Eldred Haddock' (Arthur Caddick) is depicted as a morphine addict and a drunkard, and Mrs Haddock, his wife, as a clinging encumbrance. Caddick was, as his daughter, Diana testifies, a regular user of amphetamines, legitimately prescribed by the local GP. That he was a drunkard was conceded by his own solicitors. He's here with us now and none too steady. It's like being with a caricature of someone you know. Bryan Wynter has come from his remote 'Carn' cottage above Zennor, where he lives with his wife, Suzanne Lethbridge, who funnily enough, is the daughter of Mabel Lethbridge OBE, another litigant of The Dark Monarch book. In fact, both Suzanne ('Petrouchka') and Mabel ('Maggie Bendix') are characters. Vi Morris ('Vi Gannet'), was the fourth litigant.

To me, the whole St Ives art colony and its characters were fascinating. No two days were alike, each day producing another story, a new artist discovered, a book of poems written and published, arguments between painters and galleries, who was the best sculptor, and who produced the best pottery. It was a town alive with an artistic bent that was hard to get away from if you sat anywhere near the fringe of it all. Here we were, gathered together in a group of well-known artists, writers and the daughter of a famous author and me – who was none of those things other than a couple of published poems and a tinkering jeweller.

Bryan Wynter started off by giving us an account of

why he had recently started a series of paintings based on water, explaining to the group that the meandering of water is a symbol for new life and spiritual renewal. Food for thought, while everyone took this in until Roger Hilton burst forth, in an inebriated way gesticulating that his work was superb, water or not. Tony O'Malley looked across at me, raising his eyes with a hopeless look as if to say, *I don't think we'll be talking about, or reciting our poetry today*, as Arthur Caddick took to the stage.

And no, we didn't get a look in, as the afternoon went on with a couple of red wine bottles already drunk, Sarah's offer of tea only reached Tony, Hyman, Bryan, and me. Charged with a passion all of their own, it was, nevertheless, a captivating afternoon to listen at first-hand, to the artists of the moment, who were in their fashion, putting St Ives on the map. We all agreed to meet up again in a couple of weeks to give the poets and writers a chance to discuss their work. We all said our goodbyes and thanked Sarah profusely. Tucking Tony into the passenger seat of the Sprite we set off back to St Ives, knowing in my heart – meeting again in two weeks' time was never going to happen.

A couple of guests, unknown to John, had booked into Trewyn for a few days. They arrived in the afternoon. She was a gorgeous-looking twenty-odd year old called Nicola, with blonde hair, a good figure attired in trendy jeans and a sweat-shirt. Her partner, quite the reverse, was a gentleman in his fifties, with receding hair, smallish in height, and a heavenly smile, dressed in dark trousers, a tweed jacket and a dog-collared shirt who introduced himself as, Father Brocard Sewell, a Roman Catholic Priest. The two standing together looked an unlikely couple.

Firstly, Nicola asked if it was alright that her car was parked behind the Sprite outside the garage gate entrance in Richmond Place. I said I'd take a look to make sure there was space for cars to pass as the road was quite narrow. There outside, parked neatly behind the Sprite was a white Porsche sports car – that was a surprise and a Wow-factor in St Ives. Nicola, to me, looked more like a Mini Cooper type – which just goes to show. Returning to the house, Nicola and Brocard had booked with Ivaldo to join us for dinner that evening and mentioned needing two rooms. With some relief, I showed them each to separate bedrooms and left them to settle in, thanking someone above that there happened to be another room available.

Dinner that evening was an absolute joy with Nicola enlightening us with her joie de vivre personality. She held the table with tales of her derring-do in life as well as being a successful graphic designer, based in an old art studio in Blenheim Crescent, off Portobello Road, London. She was a breath-of-fresh air and fun to be with. Brocard, as he asked us to call him, was dressed casually in chinos and a smart check shirt without the dog-collar. Remarking on this later to Brocard, as I was under the impression that priests wore them at all times, he just laughed and told me that he was not required to wear a Roman collar all the time. It was worn at his own discretion or when required by the Roman Catholic Church for certain occasions. That was me put well and truly in place.

We enjoyed the rest of the evening listening to some of Brocard Sewell's illustrious career as a British Carmelite friar and literary figure. He spoke affectionately of his friendships with Diana Mosley, Henry Williamson, and Christine Keeler, who he describes as "a beautiful and well-mannered young woman." Obviously, the level of his tolerance of human oddity was part of his extraordinary charm. He was suspended from preaching and hearing confessions in his diocese, and expelled from the Priory at Aylesford after writing a letter to The Times, protesting at the papal report on birth control. I also remarked upon the wine he was drinking and his retort being, "perhaps most of us have, at least potentially, something of the decadent in us."

Father Brocard Sewell, a small owlish man, with a quizzical but imperturbable expression is captivating, and without doubt, one of the most colourful and controversial personalities I have come across. The dinner went on forever, and there were still many questions to ask and stories to be heard. I knew deep down that their brief visit to Cornwall and St Ives would not be the last time I would see these two bright, intelligent, and inspiring people.

Soon after Nicola and Brocard left Trewyn, I had news from my sister, now living in Leicester with her family, that my brother-in-law, Neville, had been offered a work contract for a year in Cape Town, South Africa. Neville is a civil engineer, and the offer was a good position with one of the largest building contractors in the country. It was a wonderful opportunity for them, and if they liked the country and the job, it could be permanent. This, of course, hit me hard. My sister and brother-in-law together with their three children, Jonathan 10, Alison 9, and Richard 8, were a large part of my life, and the thought of them being six thousand miles away on another continent was daunting. On hearing this news, I decided to go up to see them in Leicester before they left, then on up to Manchester to see my brother Geoff, his wife Margaret, and their five children. Visiting Geoff and his family after saying goodbye to them all at my sister's would soften the blow and ease the pain somewhat before returning to Cornwall.

Before rushing off to Leicester, I had been out taking a walk along Clodgy Point. Perching on a rock and looking endlessly out to sea listening to the music of the waves, a strange gentleman walked past and nodded while not exactly looking at me, but I believe it was intended for me as there was no one else around. It was a blustery day when only the locals, it would appear, wrapped themselves up against the cold and wet to venture out against the elements of high winds and raging seas. We were the stalwarts of 'nothing like healthy fresh air to blow the cobwebs away'. I vaguely recognised the gentleman who was perhaps in his mid-to-late-thirties. Saying 'hello' in response to his nod, I got up, and together we walked back in companionable silence along the coastal path towards St Ives. By the time we reached Beach Road, I had realised it was the naïve painter, Bryan Pearce who was my walking companion. An exhibition of his paintings at the Penwith Gallery, a few years previously is where I first saw Bryan, and became an admirer of his work. A brochure and a short history of his life and art shows states he has been untouched by any formal academic teaching. Since childhood, Bryan has been affected by a rare inherited condition, phenylketonuria, that severely limited his learning and communication abilities. Bryan and I seemed to walk the same walks in and around St Ives, so we made a kind of plan to meet once a week and do a walk together – company for both of us in peace and harmony.

It was exciting getting back to St Ives after Leicester and Manchester. It was always great to see my beloved family, to reunite with my eight nieces and nephews, who seemed to be growing faster than life itself, and I loved them all. But Cornwall was my home now. The narrow cobbled streets, the glorious beaches with the high surfing waves under a blue, blue sky, the pasty shops, the art galleries, and the fishing boats bobbing merrily in the harbour, were as welcoming as anyone could possibly want. My heart was in this town, and a life away from it felt impossible. But returning came with its problems. First I was to learn that Robin had left Trewyn and was selling his cottage at Higher Stennack, and moving to Nancledra to another cottage out of the village on the road to Penzance.

This seemed quite remote to me as Robin didn't drive – the cottage was on the end of a row of cottages so he wouldn't be alone, Boots assured me when questioning her about this move. She would give him lifts whenever he needed and do his shopping. Personally, I thought this was a daft idea that would burden her – but Boots, more than anyone, knew what she was doing. *Where was his daughter Greta, in all this,* I kept asking myself? Well, I was soon to find out.

Secondly, I learned from Greta that her relationship with the potter had finished some weeks previously, now she was in love with a well-known abstract artist, whom she adored, and was pregnant with his child. The artist in question was married with a lovely wife, and he wanted Greta to have an abortion. Greta was inconsolable and wanted to keep the child. Eventually, common sense prevailed, and she had a termination. The artist dumped her like a ton of bricks, and Greta eventually went away to London.

The highlight of my return was a walk with Bryan. I dropped a note with his mother, Mary, to arrange a meeting place outside Pedn Olva Hotel as Bryan wanted to show me a walk from there across to Carbis bay and beyond. He was already there waiting when I arrived at Pedn Olva – it gave me such pleasure to be in the company of this serene and gentle man, although we said very little. Being in his company was enough, and I like to think and believe that he felt the same – though one couldn't be sure other than his face seemed to light up when he saw me. Our walks were always discovering nature, the wildflowers and the birds amongst the glorious hedgerows weaving in and out on the pathway all the way to Carbis Bay. Bryan showed me 'Little Parc Owls', the home of Peter Lanyon, set in its own lovely garden. Bryan seemed to have liked Peter a lot.

A kind of flurry hits St Ives with the arrival of the new owner of The Porthminster Hotel, Jim Prentice, together with his friends, Geraldine and Glyn Vaughan. These were young go-getters and seemed to embrace the St Ives scene with gusto, stirring up a storm in the rather, dull as ditch-water Porthminster, where, by all accounts, nobody who was anybody, stayed. In its glory days in the 1920's it was the 'Best Hotel' to stay at, close to the town and beaches with The Porthminster railway station just below. The Victorians flocked to it. Jim Prentice and his friends were about to turn Porthminster Hotel around.

Jim, a tall man in his thirties, with lank, sandy hair

and a round face was great fun, and he loved visiting Trewyn whenever he could. I think he admired the décor of the house and the ambience. But beneath everything, he was a shrewd businessman, and we soon became aware that befriending John would give him a platform into the higher echelons of St Ives society, getting to know important and well-known people with plenty of clout. Geraldine was a partner in the business sense, and Glyn was a gorgeous, blonde eighteen-year-old, who loved surfing.

Jim told us that Glyn's parents had emigrated to Australia, and Glyn didn't want to go with them, so Jim was appointed his guardian in their absence. They were a refreshing bunch – Greta re-appeared from London and quickly latched onto Jim Prentice and his rather smart car. There was no further mention of the well-known abstract artist or the pregnancy. It was intended that The Porthminster Hotel would showcase some of the St Ives artists in and around the reception and lounge areas and might even create a small art gallery on the premises.

During a walk around Smeaton's Pier and Bamaluz Beach, I decided to call into the Troika Pottery at Wheal Dream (under the Seamans' Mission) where Benny Sirota, Les Illsley (brother of Bryan, my jewellery teacher), and Stella Benjamin were busy creating away at their slab pots and mould-cast sculptural pieces influenced by Paul Klee and Brancusi. The Cycladic masks with Aztec-style decoration and the heavily-textured monolithic wares were fast becoming Troika's trademark.

The smell of the pottery was like no other, quite different from the Leach, the Arch or the Mask pottery – it had a certain evocative and earthy smell, and it always felt warm and welcoming, which may well have been from the types of material Troika used. It was altogether, a different art form of pottery inspired by Caroline Illsley and her husband, Leslie, whose idea it was to start a pottery in 1960. Caroline was the designer and Leslie did the cast pottery. Caroline's father, Sir Douglas Frank, funded the setting up of Troika in 1963 at Wheal Dream. Her brother-in-law, Roland Miller, dreamed up the trading name. Leslie and Caroline decided to take on two people: Benny Sirota and Jan Thompson, as by now they had a baby, Saskia, and Caroline was unable to work full-time.

Caroline remained the decorative artist at the pottery. They wanted to pursue their vision of pottery as art, without regard to function. Troika initially relied on the ceramics of Caroline that included the novel double egg cup. The venture rapidly became successful, gaining critical praise and high sales through a combination of the summer tourist trade and contracts with department stores such as Heal's and Liberty in London. They stocked their vases, lamp bases, tableware, tiles and wall plaques.

It gave me great pleasure to watch the progress of Troika throughout my time in St Ives, to be able to call in to see them whenever possible and enjoy a cup of coffee or tea whilst watching the works of art being created. I really didn't know any of them well; I just enjoyed the atmosphere at Troika. So it was with some surprise when Benny Sirota invited me to a party at his house in the Hamlet of Cripplesease. I'd long admired the house on the road between St Ives and Penzance, on top of the brow before The Engine Inn, and Nancledra. It is a square, old granite farmhouse seen clearly from the road, surrounded by tall trees, and I'm guessing that it might well have been part of the Cripplesease Engine House mining area.

It would be exciting to see the inside of Benny's house, and to satisfy my curiosity, so I decided to drop into the party on my way home from Trewyn back to Nancledra, and I was not disappointed. There were plenty of people there that I knew, lots of good food and, the interior of the house was stunning. Music was playing from a strange-looking piece of machinery that Benny was hovering over, and I decided to go and take a look. Admiring the steel and perspex turntable, which in itself looked like a work of art – Benny proudly told me this was his prized possession – a Bang and Olufsen sound system.

It was beautiful, and my first thought was, *Troika Pottery must be doing very well*, and I hoped that it was.

Galina Von Meck arrived as a visitor to Trewyn with a gentleman called, Bertie Pocock. Bertie Pocock hailed himself as the CEO of Hoover, Australia. He was a tall, thick-set man in his fifties, who wore good casual clothes with a nautical theme, and a blonde toupee set slightly askew. He was very dapper, quite posh with good taste and a tad on the effeminate side. Underneath all this, Bertie was a good and kind man, as one got to know him. His guest, Galina von Meck, was an extraordinary lady, to say the least. Galina was the grand-niece of the Russian composer Pyotr Tchaikovsky. She was born in Moscow; the third child of Nadezhda von Meck's son Nikolai, and Tchaikovsky's niece, Anna. She is a writer and translator. She translated the correspondence between Tchaikovsky and her grandmother into English.

On a visit to England in 1912, she met her first husband, William Noel Burrows Perrott, by whom she had a daughter, Anna (1915); he failed to settle into Russian life, and the marriage was dissolved in 1925. Galina was later arrested for trying to assist a prisoner over the Russian frontier, and spent several years in Moscow's Lubianka prison, and exile in Siberia, where she married for the second time to a fellow prisoner, Dmitrii Orlovskii, who later disappeared. She was released in 1935 and made her way to England via Germany.

If I have to single out one or two of the finest, most interesting guests at Trewyn, Galina von Meck stands way ahead in my personal poll. She was Victorianesque in her looks but quite a bit taller than the famous Monarch. With her long, grey hair pulled tightly back into a neatly coiled bun – she stood royally, a proud Russian in her mid-seventies, of gentle voice and formidable determination. She had a passionate love of her great uncle's music, and I was forever grateful that John had a superb collection of classical music, much of which was Tchaikovsky.

It was difficult to ascertain the connection between

Bertie Pocock and Galina von Meck, but there they were, two very different people – a bit like Nicola Wood and Father Brocard. But they got on well together, with Bertie taking Galina on trips around and across West Penwith. They dined in on the nights we served dinner, so the conversations were fascinating, informative, and fun. Bertie loved Australia and even suggested I go and work for him in Sydney. The temptation was great, and I did give it some serious thought. But I really did need to settle down at something, and goldsmithing was what I could do fairly well, and needed to get on with. If I failed in London, Bertie said, I could still take up his offer.

John and I often went shopping in Penzance to stock up at the Cash 'n' Carry and to also visit the rather nice delicatessen in Green Market. We usually made these trips on a Thursday, to coincide with having lunch at the Abbey Hotel in Chapel Street. The Abbey is a truly outstanding 17th century Cornish Mansion and is now home to genteel ladies of a certain age.

On Thursdays, the restaurant is open to the general public and produces a three-course meal costing the price of a starter at most other restaurants. The lunches served were nothing fancy – merely soup, a good roast meat dish (that changed every week), followed by a hearty pudding and coffee. This was served by waitresses wearing formal black dress, white apron, and a white stiff-laced headpiece – presenting the true epitome of an old-fashioned waitress from another age. The food was excellent, the waitresses were efficient, the other diners were nearly always women, thirty to forty years older than us and we loved it. Abbey days were fun, just listening to the next tables' conversations made a visit there worthwhile.

Chapel Street itself is steeped in history. Number 25 is where Maria Branwell lived – she was the mother of Charlotte, Anne, Emily, and Branwell Bronte. The most colourful building on the street is the Admiral Benbow pub, named after the 17th century Admiral, John Benbow. It is also famed for being in the opening scene of Treasure

Island by Robert Louis Stevenson. There's a statue of a smuggler lying astride the roof, musket in hand.

The Turks Head Pub in Chapel Street is reputedly the oldest pub in the town. In the 1820's, the pub was run by a Holloway, who was the father of the Victorian entrepreneur and philanthropist, Thomas Holloway. When he died, he left £700,000 to build the Holloway College in Surrey. Royal Holloway College was officially opened in 1886 by Queen Victoria as an all-women college. John and I revelled in the history of the places we visited, trying to take in at least a couple of historical landmarks on our shopping trips to Penzance, Truro, or even as far afield as Plymouth.

Our friends Johnny and Toops have recently opened a restaurant in New Street, Penzance, which they have called, Bistro One. Neither Johnny or Toops have had restaurant experience before, but somehow they are making a success of it. Boots and I enjoyed eating at the small, intimate and cosy Bistro, where we've whiled away many a night. We enjoyed good food and listening to Jose Feliciano pouring his heart out with 'California Dreamin', 'Light My Fire', 'Don't Let the Sun Catch You Crying', and other tracks from his 1968 album 'Feliciano' that was all the rage in Cornwall.

Another new restaurant opened in Penzance by two male friends of Boots, called 'Camelot', in Alverton Street. Being quite a connoisseur of good food and restaurants, Boots was often invited to the opening night of a new eaterie, which she always refused to attend. On asking her the reason for this, she said it was not the correct thing to do because if you didn't enjoy the food, the ambience or anything else, it was difficult to say so, being a guest. It was better to be a paying customer and voice your opinion objectively if it was requested.

My personal favourite restaurant was 'The Lobster Pot' in Mousehole, where I first went with Cosmo and Victor, when they were visiting Trewyn, and sometimes after, with Boots or John, and Brian Smith. This great restaurant, serving the best lobster and crab as well as the fish catches of the day, sat overlooking the small fishing harbour, and was to me, a knockout. Their Crab Gratin or Lobster Thermidor served with a chilled glass of Sauvignon Blanc set the taste buds quivering. Visits to 'The Lobster Pot', did not, alas, happen often. As for Mousehole itself, Dylan Thomas called it "quite the loveliest village in England"... enough said.

When Ivaldo couldn't get fresh fish from St Ives, he would ask me to go to the fish wholesalers in Newlyn early in the morning in order to obtain fresh fish, for dinner that evening. It was another world arriving at the cold storage warehouses as the catches were brought in ready for packing. This was truly where the real lifeline of the Cornish fishing industry lay. The early morning hustle and bustle as box after box of fish were deposited at the cold storage warehouses, was a sight and experience to behold. The camaraderie and the joshing between the warehouse staff and the fishermen were in a language only known to them – it was alive!

Buying fish directly from these wholesalers was, in itself, an art form. Mackerel, pilchards, cod, hake, and monkfish would be slapped and wrapped onto large sheets of paper, then wrapped again in newspaper, always chatting, and a cheery smile. I often just took a large, stainless steel-lidded catering pan that they'd throw the fish into on a bed of ice – especially in the warmer months, for safer transportation back to St Ives. Going to the fish markets in Newlyn was special, as was buying fresh fish from the fishermen on Smeaton's Pier.

The Newlyn Society of Artists is as impressive as the Penwith Gallery or The St Ives Society of Artists. Tony O'Malley needed to visit the Newlyn Art Gallery, so I gave him a lift over there one afternoon, and I was really impressed. Ploughing through the history of The Newlyn School, it was thrilling to see pioneers of the art world who had been associated with the school. Stanhope Forbes, Laura Knight, Lamorna Birch, Alfred Munnings to name but a few, and more recent – our very own; Terry Frost, Patrick Heron, Peter Lanyon, Bernard Leach, John Wells, and Wilhelmina Barnes-Graham – together the St Ives and Newlyn Society of Artists' members read like a Who's Who of the Art World.

There is a good Fisherman's Co-operative Store not far from the Newlyn Art Gallery, and we trudged along to see if there were any nice sweaters, smocks or jackets suitable for Tony in preparation of the upcoming winter. This store has absolutely everything for the nautical seafarer and the artists alike – they all seem to favour the obligatory navy blue smocks, the Aran and the Guernsey sweaters. A bit like a traditional Cornish uniform, it was hard sometimes to differentiate between the fishermen and the artists. In the winter, the uniform was topped with a sou'wester coat and a woollen beanie pulled over the head to keep warm out of the wind and rain. We found a navy Guernsey that fitted Tony nicely and some warm woollen socks. Happy with his new purchases, we set off back to St Ives via the Army Surplus Store in Hayle, where he was now in search of blankets for his studio at Porthmeor.

Throughout our trip to Newlyn, Tony was a bit on the thoughtful side, so much so that I questioned him about it. Apparently, Boots had been suggesting that Tony should marry his girlfriend, Jane Harris. Tony had never been married before and seemed wary about the prospect. He was nearly sixty, and Jane was half his age, and he worried about that, as well as his health, the future, and felt himself in a quandary what to do for the best.

There was no doubt that they loved each other very much, and I felt for my dear friend. Jane was good for him, and he was good for Jane – and at the age they both were it seemed logical for them to get married and I told him so. Boots had been absolutely right in her machinations of this – Jane would look after Tony in his twilight years, and she would have security with him. Underneath it all, Tony knew all of this but somehow needed to have assurance from the friends whom he cared about, and who cared about him. I dropped a more cheerful Tony off at Porthmeor Studios and made my way back to Nancledra in the knowledge that sometime in the near future, Tony would pop the question.

Arriving back at Heather Cottage, all seemed in darkness with the outside lights turned on and the Bassett Hounds barking away behind the kitchen door. Letting myself in and the dogs out, the kitchen greeted me warmly from the AGA and a note on the large round table from Boots telling me she had gone to the Leach Pottery for a business dinner with Janet. I made myself some supper; let the dogs back in and started reading my latest Winston Graham book, 'Warleggan'. I loved these Winston Graham novels, primarily because they are written about Cornwall in the very area surrounding me: Nancledra, Zennor and the dramatic cliffs overlooking the Atlantic, and the wild moors around us. He writes of Ross Poldark, the family feuds, of smugglers, tin mining, skulduggery, and passion way back in another era. Winston Graham, born in Manchester, moved to Perranporth in Cornwall when he was a teenager and wrote the first Poldark novel in 1945. He has captivated his readers ever since with these dramatic novels.

I was deep into George Warleggan when Boots arrived back from having dinner with Janet, and not in the best of moods. In fact, she was in a foul mood and despairing. It was supposed to have been a business meeting she told me. But Janet had been drinking before she arrived and by the time they sat down to eat she was already drunk. Boots had refused to listen to her garbled arguments about nothing, until Boots was totally fed up and started to leave, whereupon Janet lashed out at her in verbal, vitriolic abuse. Eventually Boots managed to extricate herself from Janet and make her way down the Studio steps to her car and drive quickly away. It was not the first time that this had happened, and I reminded Boots of this. There seemed little point in making excuses 'it was the drink', "it's happening more frequently, and one of these days you'll come to blows and then what?" I asked her.

Boots soaked in the bath for a while to calm down and regain her composure, promising herself to do something serious about the situation during the next few days. Janet was besotted with Boots, that was clear – when she finally realised the feeling was not reciprocated . . . Janet drowned her sorrows in bourbon.

After seven years of living in St Ives, I knew it was time for me to move on. It was time for me to move on if I wanted to become a goldsmith. Heart breaking as it would be to leave my beloved village, I was not going to get far at being successful in Cornwall – I needed more training, more experience if I wanted to get to exhibition, showroom, or gallery standard. Once I'd mastered the craft successfully, I kept telling myself, I could return to St Ives and open a studio. Until then, there was nothing to do but move forward, and London, without doubt, was the place to achieve great things.

The situation with Boots and her partnership with Janet was not improving. It hurt me tremendously to see someone as knowledgeable, kind, and encouraging as Boots was with artists, craftsmen, potters, and jewellers that she introduced to the New Craftsman, being treated in this manner. She had made it into one of the best art galleries in St Ives. When I told Boots of my decision to leave and try my luck in London, she was delighted. We'd discussed it many times, but I couldn't bring myself to leave, being harboured in my comfort zone. Brian Illsley was even more helpful and encouraging, so from there, I made plans to leave Cornwall in the next couple of months.

It was the end of the season and an appropriate time to let John and Ivaldo know that I would be leaving. My time at Trewyn had run its course in a natural way. John seemed to be spending more time in London than in Cornwall. Ivaldo was threatening more often than not that he was leaving John, and returning home to Italy. It had been a great experience for me working at Trewyn, learning about good cooking, fine wines, classical music, opera, and entertaining. Above all, I learned a lot about art, sculpture, pottery, and jewellery, not only from being at Trewyn but by living amongst this great colony of artists, craftsmen, writers and poets in St Ives. Giving me a wealth of knowledge I would never have had sitting behind a desk doing accountancy. Being in St Ives Where the Light Is, surrounded by the sun, the sea, the sky, and the endless golden beaches where the surf pounds upon its shores in waves of frothy white spume. It's where I've swum with the tides, and attempted to surf in the wild Atlantic Ocean that I love so much.

Rob and Owen have sold their Outrigger Restaurant and moved to London. Having heard that I was moving to London, they've phoned and said that I can stay with them when I first arrive, for which I'm very grateful and relieved. My plan was to get a bed-sitter in Kensington Garden Square, Bayswater, where I've stayed with Carol on the odd trip to the capital, and the rooms are quite spacious, for one it would be perfect. However, money was scarce and what little I'd managed to save was not going to last too long paying rent. It was a daunting feeling, and it felt like I was taking a quantum leap into the abyss. But press on I would. Money from private sales of my jewellery I'd put back into buying silver and investing in some good, but expensive, German jewellers tools. At least I had enough to start making jewellery once I'd found a niche in which to start.

John and Bill were also thinking of selling their news agency, Watson and Jones, and moving off to go and live in Spain. It had been a cracking business, and the boys had made it into a lovely shop. But it was hard, hard work and the hours were killing them, from 06.00 hrs in the morning (newspaper deliveries to the shop), until 20.00 hrs in the evening. Neither of them liked leaving the shop, so they each took it in turns to be there with a couple of their staff – which meant they never got time together to enjoy their lovely home at Towednack. I would miss these two a lot as I'd known John from way back in Manchester – but eh! Life goes on, upward, and onward. They were still pretty young, and I doubted St Ives would have been enough for them in the end. They were hard-working guys who would make a success at whatever they put their minds to. My weekly visits to get the compulsory, St Ives Times and Echo in Watson and Jones, would be sorely missed.

Chapter Ten

As Tears Go By

Robin, now living in Nancledra, became quite ill and Boots spent a lot of time keeping an eye him, doing his shopping, and making sure he was eating well. Greta was somewhere living in London, near Westminster. It was a sad time for me as Robin and I had been good friends since I arrived in St Ives – good buddies, lots of fun and laughter and more so when he worked at Trewyn. Somewhere deep inside me, I had a feeling that Robin would not be with us for much longer, and my heart ached for him. There was little that I could do to help, that Boots was not already doing, so I'd call in and chat to him or sit quietly, and just be there.

A trip was needed to go to Hayle, and say my farewells to Betty. I hardly ever saw her these days but heard the news that she was doing quite well writing songs for the newly formed progressive rock band 'Renaissance'. Betty's friend was the lead vocalist Jane Relf, and Jane's brother Keith Relf was vocalist and lead guitarist. I personally wasn't into the Renaissance music, so I knew little of the band other than Keith being an ex-Yardbirds band member. I was pleased things were happening for Betty, and knowing above all that she was a good writer, I was sure she'd go far in the music world.

Betty had moved from the Hayle estuary bungalow by Old Quay House and was living in a flat opposite the shops in Foundry Square. Life seemed to have improved for Betty and Liz, for one thing being away from the estuary and its dampness was a good move. Things were beginning to look up, they told me, as Betty's song writing was getting accepted and aired. She still looked very pale and wan, but I think that was the nature of the beast. The roll-ups were still being smoked, the smile was still there, as well as the humour, and it was good to see Betty in an upbeat frame of mind since our first encounter in the dole queue all those years ago. We hadn't really remained friends, but we had a connection neither of us knew much about – but something was there that kept us in touch. I bade my farewell to Betty and Liz, promising to write if I didn't get the chance to see them before I left Cornwall. It was a sad departure from Hayle back to St Ives.

Not being in the mood for a party, as John suggested, an idea came from Tony and Jane to have something at the St Ives Arts Club – a get-together of friends making use of the gallery downstairs and the little theatre upstairs. It was conveniently central on Westcott's Quay so that nobody had to drive. *The grandeur of Trewyn*, I thought, *might have been intimidating to some of my friends who would not be able to let their hair down as easily as they could at the Arts Club*. There was no leaving date as yet, so we had a month or two to arrange this farewell get-together. Heather Jameson, who had dumped the formidable Gary for someone else, offered Hanter Chy to have a party, but again, the Arts Club was neutral and the best all-round for everyone and a donation from me for the venue would help the Arts Club coffers.

Poor Robin died, leaving Boots and me very, very sad. He became so sick in the end that it was a relief to see the suffering end. Greta came down from London and descended on us in a drama of inconsolable tears and heartbreak. Boots let her stay at Heather Cottage so she wouldn't be on her own in her father's cottage up the road. Big hot fires, warm baths and good wholesome food were what Boots described as 'Doctors Orders' for bereavement. Two weeks later, Greta was still at Heather Cottage sitting around in her father's huge, long, heavy dressing gown that she'd insisted upon wearing from the moment she arrived and would not take off – the sight and sound of Greta was beginning to wear thin, and Boots realised that she would have to do something about it.

It's not as if Greta had been particularly close to her

father – her behaviour had indeed hinted otherwise. In all the homes that Robin had lived in during my time in St Ives, the rooms were festooned in photographs of Greta in silver, gilt or wooden frames on every surface imaginable. I once asked Robin why he had so many photographs of Greta around the place. He replied with a huge grunt and a laugh that Greta had put the photographs of herself in the frames and placed them strategically on Robin's fine pieces of antique furniture and the mantelpiece. I was flabbergasted when he told me this – not one photograph of anyone else in their home – just of Greta.

Eventually, she did leave and all got back to normal at Heather Cottage. Robin's cottage was sold, and all his affairs were sorted out and put in order. Greta eventually returned to London and the flat in Westminster which she shared with three others. We did feel sorry for her, as there did not appear to be any other family whatsoever. Robin's financial situation did not leave Greta with anything much once everything had been settled – it was a sad situation. But our lives have been richer, having known Robin, and we were grateful for that.

It was the end of the season, and John was having a one-man exhibition at the Marjorie Parr Gallery in London sometime towards Christmas. He had been working hard throughout the year for the exhibition, and the tension arising from this, with plaster cast sculptures getting to the foundry late for casting or being returned not quite to John's satisfaction was pretty mind-blowing for anyone around him. After some discussions and mutual consent between us, John decided to close Trewyn to visitors until the season started the following year. Ivaldo was pretty choked off and upset, whilst I felt pleased that my position was not being filled in case all went awry in London. John said I was welcome to leave the Frogeye Sprite in the garage with the Mercedes until I found somewhere safe in London to keep it.

Being grateful to John for that, I gathered my clothes together, packed up the Sprite and left for Nancledra with a promise from John that we'd have a celebratory dinner together at a new Italian restaurant he'd discovered near Carn Brea Castle, in Redruth.

Not letting the grass grow under my feet, Jim Prentice phoned me at Heather Cottage and asked if I'd help them out at The Porthminster Hotel, as a lot of the seasonal staff had already left and they had a couple of new conference bookings. So off I went to work at The Porthminster for a couple of weeks. Jim hadn't mentioned on the phone what my job description would be – perhaps better not on his part or I would never have agreed to help out. General factotum was exactly what I got paid to do, from reception, chambermaid, waitress, and washing up – those were my duties. However, on a good note, beautiful Glyn was working there, and we got on well together and became close friends. When we managed to scratch some time, we would go to Porthmeor Beach where I could watch him cresting the waves and pick up some hints on how to surf properly.

One day, when the weather had turned to wind, rain, and stormy seas, it was hopeless to spend time at the beach, Glyn asked me to his flat for the evening to listen to some Beach Boys music – might as well as we can't do any surfing he'd suggested. I was on duty all day and told him so, but would let him know when I finished if I'd join him. For the rest of the day, I was in a quandary what to do. Glyn had a room in the flat which he shared with Jim Prentice and Geraldine, further up the road from The Porthminster. He'd mentioned that Jim and Geraldine were away on business and he was alone. Bells rang, and sirens sounded all day long knowing that I really did want to spend the evening with Glyn, but something inside kept telling me it was the wrong thing to do.

In the end, and with every fibre of my being, I did not join Glyn that evening. This decision changed our friendship somewhat and soon after, but sadly, I left The Porthminster. Regrets? Yes, there were regrets, being a touch in love with each other was not what we wanted.

Better to leave as we were, and walk away.

The balmy nights at The Count House Folk Music Club at Botallack, would be sorely missed. Not that we went there all that often, logistically being a tad too far along the coast road, especially at night. I'd miss Brenda Wootton, John the Fish, Tel Mann, and sometimes the indomitable Pete Chatterton. It would be really special to have one last blast of folk music at The Count House, with a group of friends – maybe I could persuade Boots' son, Nick Redgrave, to come down from London to join us and sing a few of his folk songs at The Count House, to make it a special evening together with Boots, Jackie and a few of her surfing friends, Carol, Norman Stocker, Brian Smith, Tony and Jane and perhaps even Roger and Rose Hilton as they lived so near. I made a mental note to get the ball rolling as soon as possible, as it was never easy letting people know and then getting them all together, was another mission.

One thing that had needled me since arriving in St Ives was the lack of ever meeting the reclusive, classical composer, Priaulx Rainier. I tried to get my head around what somebody who was reclusive did all the time – in this case, I presume she dedicated her life to composing music. After all, she wrote compositions for the cellist, Jacqueline du Pre, and the violinist, Yehudi Menuhin. But surely she went out at some time or another, did shopping, went for a walk or maybe for a swim in the beautiful ocean surrounding her – for inspiration perhaps? Priaulx Rainier was a complete enigma, and invitations from people such as Boots, John, and Janet Leach were always met with a polite but firm, no thank you.

However, according to Brian Smith, she did visit her friend Barbara Hepworth frequently at Trewyn Studio, when she was in residence at her home in St Ives, tucked away at the top of Tregenna Steps. Priaulx apparently, I was to learn, having been in St Ives for the last couple of months, had returned to her home in London so there was little hope of my ever seeing or meeting her, as I would be long gone before she returned to St Ives again.

During the next three weeks, I made a point of visiting friends at the Troika Pottery, Anthony and Christiane Richards at Penderleath Pottery, up on Crippleseaase, John Buchanan (brother of my friend, Mary Buchanan) at Anchor Pottery in Hayle. John and Mary's mother lived in a lovely chalet on Hayle Towans, with a long stretch of beach and the turquoise Atlantic on her doorstep – wow, how I envied her. There was nobody at the Leach Pottery to say goodbye to as I didn't know Bill Marshall and Trevor Corser, who were still working there as well as Bernard and Janet Leach – others I'd befriended, apprentices mostly, had been and gone. In fact, there were a lot of changes afoot in the local pottery world. The Mask Pottery and the Val Bakers had moved from St Christopher's on Porthmeor to the Old Sawmills at Golant on the river Fowey. The Richard's had moved from the Arch Pottery at Hicks Court to the Penderleath at Crippleseaase, and John Buchanan from the Arch Pottery to his new, Anchor Pottery, in Hayle.

The smell of each different pottery makes me feel nostalgic, and I haven't left Cornwall yet. It's the clay, the potter's wheel turning in moulding, artistic hands, the glazes, the heat of the kilns and the all-engrossing atmosphere are some things that will remain in my memory. In winter, when the storms lash the sea over the wall of Lambeth Walk, and the Wharf, making it impossible to venture outside – the warm comfort of a snug pottery is always a welcome refuge.

Every day I am finding the thought of leaving St Ives harder, heartbreakingly harder. I want to say goodbye to everyone and thank them for their friendship, a bit daft, but it's just how I feel. I haven't told Bryan {Pearce} yet that I shall be leaving – I get too choked up just thinking about it. He deserves more than anyone to know, and in my head, I've planned a walk to Clodgy, from where we can see The Garrack Hotel, and across Porthmeor to the Island where we'll walk after we leave Clodgy Point. I made a firm resolution to drop a note with Bryan's mother, Mary, to arrange when a walk would suit Bryan.

Spending an afternoon around Porthmeor, and the Penwith Gallery, was always a pleasant experience as you never knew who you'd find in the studios that were always busy with creativity. One artist would be visiting another, drinking tea and coffee, or even enjoying a beer – there was always a sense of camaraderie which overrode the competition between them, and that was good to see. I once found the amazing painter, Sandra Blow, having a chat in one of the studios with Patrick Heron and Willie Barnes-Graham – she was on one of her frequent visits to St Ives. Being a great admirer of her large abstract canvases, it was overwhelming to meet her and spend time in her company.

The Mariners' Church, home of the St Ives Society of Artists, stands out proud and towers above the rest of the smaller buildings around it. This Church is a majestic monument to both the local fishermen and now to the St Ives Society of Artists. It has been the subject of much controversy between the hierarchy of the local art colony since the death of Borlase Smart, secretary of the society from 1933, and its later President, who was the driving force behind its early success.

The Mariners' Church commands a central location that can be seen from almost every vantage point. It is also a central location in the story of the artists' colony. Standing proudly next to Norway Square, I decide to visit the latest exhibition, and I'm glad that I have as it's very impressive. The quality of art produced in St Ives always amazed me. This former Church building is a huge space to display in, but it is covered in a myriad of stunning artworks before me as I meander around in awe, thinking, *how I shall miss all this on my doorstep.*

There are not many people in the gallery, so I have a chance to chat to the curator, who I vaguely know, and she tells me that the summer season is coming to an end and visitors to the gallery are getting less and less every day, and it's a long winter ahead to get through. Well, that's the nature of the beast, I remind her – St Ives is a seasonal holiday destination, and once the sun's gone down, the tourists depart. Wishing her a bonne farewell, I leave and make my way back to the little green Sprite parked in Richmond Place, outside Trewyn.

For reasons unknown, the desire to visit Zennor was strong, so I made my way out there one fine morning, planning to visit Sarah Williamson at the Old Poor House on the way back. I've loved Zennor from the moment I first went there in the early days of my arrival in St Ives. The walk to Zennor Head felt nostalgic being the most beautiful scenic walk that I have ever experienced with the dramatic cliffs overlooking the indigo blue ocean crashing below as the waves hurl against the rocky shoreline. Wisps of wildflowers, blues, pinks and yellow still decked the lichen-covered outcrops of rock, although the summer was over, giving the rugged, barren landscape a soft and gentle hue. I've stood upon these rocks so many times, being drawn to them and the vastness of the ocean beyond like a magnet. It is here that a lump comes into my throat, and tears spill down my cheeks unashamedly.

The thought of leaving St Ives is getting harder and harder, and now I'm thinking perhaps that I should just go and forget about all the heart-breaking goodbyes prolonging the inevitable. Back at the Tinner's Arms, the only pub in the small hamlet of Zennor, I have a bowl of pea and ham soup with warm crusty bread, which I eat outside at one of the rustic tables, and think about how lovely it is just sitting here. The Tinner's Arms is a Grade II-listed traditional Cornish Inn, the name deriving from the Tinner's, with records of tin extraction in the area dating back to Tudor times. D.H. Lawrence stayed for a fortnight in the pub in 1916.

A few short steps away from the Tinner's is the Church of Saint Senara. It is dedicated to the local saint, Saint Senara, and is at least 1400 years old and is a Grade 1 listed building. One of only two remaining bench-ends in the church portrays the Mermaid of Zennor, depicted admiring herself in a mirror. This is on the 'Mermaid Chair' which also has carvings of fish on the seat, and is believed to be at least 600 years old. The church is surrounded by a small circular graveyard, the boundaries of which have existed since the Bronze Age, and in which parish residents have been buried for centuries. Zennor Head, and the Neolithic tomb, Zennor Quoit, received her name indirectly.

Heading out of Zennor, I make a promise that I will realise that dream, and one day buy a cottage there. I decide also not to visit Sarah, another farewell is adding to the burden, and my rather weepy self should stay alone. Tomorrow I'm going to the shore shelters to seek out Seth and some of the other fishermen, and that will be a hard call. Driving back to Nancledra through Towednack is another heart-wrench, as I pass closely by John and Bill's lovely Cornish cottage, and think of the many happy times spent there.

Arriving at Heather Cottage, Boots is in the kitchen rummaging up something for dinner at the AGA, and a fire is crackling nicely in the low ceilinged sitting room. All is warm and welcoming with the Basset hounds running around, waiting for dark and the promise of escape from the confines of the garden, to chase after other beasties throughout the night. This, of course, was going to be the hardest to leave – Boots, the Bassett hounds, a warm welcoming kitchen, my jewellery workshop, even Jackie calling in from time to time (she was now living with Mike Carr in Penzance) would all be missed.

Shore Shelter day has arrived, and I've ordered some pasties from Ferrell's bakery in Fore Street, to share with my fisherman friends. I managed the evening before to phone Seth and told him to contact as many of the fishermen that he could and tell them to be at Shamrock Shelter the following day at 12 noon. It was a coolish day with a stiff breeze whipping off the water on the harbour front, so a great surprise it was to see ten fishermen squeezed into Shamrock when I walked in with warm pasties in hand. How happy I felt to be amongst these characters with sea and fishing running through their veins, with faces worn from constantly changing weather conditions out at sea, from earning a living in rough times. But I wouldn't change any one of them for the world – I spoke their language, enjoyed their company, laughed at their jokes, and best of all, they seemed to like me. We spent a couple of wonderful hours in Shamrock, while I explained to them why I would be leaving. Although sympathetic, not one of them wanted me to go, and Willie Craze even suggested I take to sea with them and become a fisherman. Heart-warming and appealing as that proposition sounded, I seriously felt that becoming a fisherman at this stage in my life was not going to get me very far into a career, as the local fishing industry was heading into serious decline. However, I thanked them all kindly, as we joked about me becoming a fisherman, and what folk would think about that. It was a good get-together, and it ended with them inviting me for a drink at the Sloop Inn, later that evening.

The Snug Bar in the Sloop was quite bustling when I arrived, and eight of the ten fishermen were there in their usual corner, including Seth. I stood with my half-pint of bitter shandy and talked with the men like true comrades as they sucked on their pipes and smoked cigarettes in a motley group, behaving like locals. Other people in the pub were sitting at the long tables enjoying their drinks and looking like tourists. It wouldn't be long now before this bar would be empty in the evenings when bar skittles would resume and life at the local would be as it should be for the fishermen.

At one end of the long tables, I spotted a couple of girls, perhaps my own age that were enjoying a drink and laughing together. One of them came up to the bar to refresh their drinks and, standing next to me, she apologised for interrupting, before asking a couple of questions about potteries in St Ives. She introduced herself as Sally and suggested that I might like to join them at the table if and when it was convenient. The boys at the bar wouldn't stay too long as their wives would be waiting with supper ready, and there'd be trouble if they lingered too long in the Sloop.

After our group dwindled down to three, I made my way over to Sally at the long table, where she introduced me to her friend, Sandy, a stunningly good-looking young lady. They told me about opening a craft shop in London and were in St Ives to look at different potteries that might supply them with pots both standard ware and art pottery. I gave them a few pointers of which potteries to visit, and they seemed happy with that – saving Sally and Sandy time, not approaching potteries that might be too expensive or too artistic for the purpose. We chatted for a bit as I really enjoyed their enthusiasm and company – it was a refreshing change. Travelling back to Heather Cottage that evening, there was a spring in my step as if a mighty load had been lifted off me. Suddenly, London did not feel so daunting.

Fate has its way of sorting things out when a few days later I was walking down Fore Street on my way to Porthmeor via The Digey, for a swim, when I bumped into Sally and Sandy outside Ferrell's bakery. They seemed thrilled to see me and to let me know how they'd got on since our meeting in the Sloop. It appeared that they'd done very well indeed, and had got themselves some good standard pottery ware, coffee mugs, coffee pots, plates, and jugs as well as a few pieces of more decorative, vases and bowls. They seemed mighty chuffed with their purchases and were heading back to London.

Then, out of the blue, Sally suggested if I wanted a lift to London, I could go with them. She had a flat in Elgin Crescent, near Portobello Rd where I could camp down for a couple of days until I sorted something out. They were leaving the following day, and they would come and pick me and my luggage up in Nancledra. I could not believe my good fortune – but, twenty-four hours to get everything together seemed insane. Being half-packed anyway; I decided there and then that this was an opportunity not to be missed, and told both girls that I would be ready and gave them directions how to get to Heather Cottage.

When Boots finished at the Craftsmen Gallery that afternoon, I returned with her to Nancledra, having left the Sprite safely in John's garage at Trewyn as he had agreed. Once I was settled in London, I would come back for it. Strangely enough, there seemed little to pack, and I was pleasantly surprised once the all-important jewellery tools and the pieces of ivory were carefully wrapped – they also took up little space. My prized possession, the Wilhelmina Barnes-Graham painting which I had, at long last, managed to buy would remain at Heather cottage until I found a place of my own in which to live. That evening, Boots and I had lobster and a few glasses of wine and talked about the future. I'd come back to Heather Cottage as many times as possible, and she would visit London as frequently as she could. There was nothing further afoot we could plan – Boots was embroiled with the Newcraftsman, and making that a success, whilst I had to find my niche in the world of goldsmithing and jewellery making. The future suddenly felt challenging.

I lay away half the night with anticipation and excitement. This was the best way for things to happen for me – immediately and without preamble. But what about Bryan and our walk, what about the arranged party at The Arts Club. I haven't said goodbye to everyone yet, and tomorrow I would be gone. This was hurting more than anything, but I could write to Bryan, and all the other artists, craftsmen, and fishermen who had become friends and explain the sudden departure, and after all, I'd be back before anyone had even missed me.

With my mind drifting back to the day I first arrived in St Ives to work at The Copper Kettle. The beatniks used to sit in circles on the beaches at night, strumming their guitars and singing anti-war songs by Leonard Cohen, Bob

Dylan, Joan Baez, with the shadow of the moon encircling them. It was eerie, beautiful, and poetic, and later as the night drew on – they got a little out of tune. Flower Power took over from beatniks, and a festoon of 'San Francisco' flowers in your hair pervaded – brightly coloured clothes, tie-dye t-shirts, paper flowers, hash, love and peace slogans, The Doors' psychedelic rock music and the Hippie era was born. Wow! How privileged I have been to have lived through this time in St Ives, Bohemian, Beatnik, Flower Power, and Hippie, in a place Where the Light Is.

Sally and Sandy arrived at Heather Cottage the next morning around 10.30 a.m. and collected me, bags and all, with no time for fuss, no time for tears and no long goodbyes. It was now or never as the car reversed and went up the small slope and onto the lane above. Looking back, I could see Boots walking towards the kitchen door, a bevy of Bassett hounds following. My heart stopped as I choked back the tears. I turned in my seat and looked straight ahead as the car sped on for the long journey to London.

Chapter Eleven

St Ives 2019

Having relived my time in St Ives during the 1960s in the previous chapters, I am now curious to discover where many of the painters, potters, writers, poets and all the other wonderful characters, might be now. I am back in the quirky flat and happy to be here since discovering that the flat is almost next to the flat above the butcher's shop that belonged to Bryan Pearce's father, Walter, and the very place where Bryan was born. I'd loved it from the moment I set foot in the flat a year ago, and now I know why. Somehow Bryan's presence is here, and I find great comfort in that.

I never did see Bryan again. On the brief times that I returned to St Ives it was never possible to meet, and somehow I felt my returning presence might be disruptive to him. Sadly he died in St Ives 11th January 2007, aged 77, but he remains with me always. Doing many walks in and around St Ives almost every single day, he is there alongside me – the quiet presence of this gentle man. Whenever the need arises to see some of Bryan's work, his naive paintings so painstakingly done to capture the town that he loved so much in every brushstroke, there are galleries that still show his work and prints are available. Of course, my greatest pleasure is seeing my beloved Bryan's original paintings on permanent show at the mighty, Tate St Ives Museum – that seriously brings a smile to my face in admiration.

The Barbara Hepworth Museum and Sculpture Garden is a stone's throw away from the flat and remains almost the same as it did in the 1960s when we walked past it every day. The Palais de Danse diagonally across the road from the museum, where my friend, Norman Stocker worked on the sculpture prototypes to be cast in bronze for Barbara's major commissions, has changed internally. But the outside of the building remains exactly the same. The former cinema and dance hall was the renowned sculptor's biggest workspace. She bought it in 1961. The former workshop has been given to The Tate St Ives by her family. She lived in Trewyn Studios from 1949 until her death, caused by a fire, at Trewyn Studio one evening in 1975. It was opened as the Barbara Hepworth Museum and Sculpture Garden a year later.

It is so interesting to discover that when I left St Ives all those years ago, I was reading through the twelve 'Poldark' novels by Winston Graham (from my home town, Manchester). Today, St Ives is a-buzz with the BBC television adaptation of 'Poldark', being filmed in and around St Ives and other parts of Cornwall. It's causing a sensation, and visitors are flocking here in their droves. German tourists especially, come over in coach loads just to see the locations. I remember watching the original series in 1975 when Robin Ellis played the heart throb, Ross Poldark. I believe the series lasted until 1977. Today, we have the handsome Aidan Turner, another heartthrob, playing Ross Poldark, and the series seems to be going on forever. Loved it then, and love it now.

With great sadness, I learn about the death of my friend, Phil Moran. I saw Phil last year at his cottage in St Andrews Street. He was very poorly, and my heart went out to him, thinking of the vibrant young man that I once knew, and brother of dear Jacque Moran. A Master Mariner, Captain Philip Moran, tall and slim, with a lovely smile capturing his clear blue eyes, and nearly always an enhancing blue shirt to match and his easy lanky walk and resonant voice, He worked with the government and was the launching authority for the St Ives Lifeboat.

Phil became an author late in life, creating his first book 'Soggy the Bear'. This, being a great success, led to the creation of a further five Soggy adventure books. His long-standing friendship with the illustrator, Michael Foreman evolved into a professional collaboration as

Phil's words and experiences provide the real-life basis for Soggy's adventures, which Michael brings to visual life through his beautiful illustrations. How I love these children's books, and how proud I am of Captain Phil. I will miss his cheery wave this year that I got each and every day in 2018, as I walked past his window – he got a right Royal St Ives send-off. RIP my friend.

Donovan Philips Leitch was born on the 10th May 1946. The Scottish singer, songwriter and guitarist of folk, jazz, pop and psychedelia music played all those years ago in the Sugar 'n' Spice. His sounds even today, take me straight back behind the Gaggia coffee machine, listening to Donovan's easy style as he sang away, strumming his guitar in between drinking coffee and eating a slice of cake. The café would be packed if news got out that he was in there with his friend and manager, Gypsy Dave. It took all our resources to keep up with the volume, and we would work flat out for a couple of hours, but it was always worth it.

At other times, Donovan could be found on the harbour or Porthmeor Beach being filmed. Emerging from the British folk scene, Donovan reached fame in the United Kingdom in early 1965, with live performances on the pop TV series Ready Steady Go! His most successful singles were the early UK hits 'Catch the Wind' in 1965. In September 1966 "Sunshine Superman" followed by 'Mellow Yellow' and in 1968 'Hurdy Gurdy Man'. He became a friend of pop musicians Joan Baez, Brian Jones, and The Beatles. He taught John Lennon a finger-picking guitar style in 1968 that Lennon employed in 'Dear Prudence', 'Julia', 'Happiness is a Warm Gun' and other songs. He was inducted into the *Rock and Roll Hall of Fame* in 2012 and the Songwriters Hall of Fame in 2014. He lives with his family in County Cork.

Gyp Mills, better known as Gypsy Dave, road manager and companion of Donovan, is a British poet, songwriter, and sculptor who now teaches and works out of studios in Thailand and Greece, and has exhibited his breathtaking bronze and marble statues worldwide. Recalling the early days, he says he and Don still find that those early days, regardless of what has happened to them since, were the best days of their lives. They were poor, they had nothing, and they had no worries. They wanted to live life, see what it was all about and talk about what they considered the important things in life. Gypsy Dave lives in Thailand in a condominium right by the sea that reminds him of somewhere in Devon and Cornwall. He wrote 'Knights of the Road', The Autobiography of Gypsy Dave Mills – His Remarkable Adventures During The 1960s With Donovan.

Heather Jameson and her teenage children, Peter, Julia, and eventually a friend of Peter's left St Ives and moved all the way to Hawaii. Julia had moved there some years previously, now Heather was going. I met her briefly in Penzance in 1985, looking exactly as she had done in 1965, with her flamboyant smiling face, happy as a sandboy living in Hawaii and about to marry the friend of Peter's who had upped from St Ives and left for pastures greener with his friends, who were about to become his family.

Owen Olver and Rob Brown sold their business, the Outrigger Restaurant, in Street-an-Pol and moved to London. Owen had played his part in the Revolution clothes shop that he opened with Caroline Illsley in the mid-sixties. He made it a great success as people got their wires crossed because of the name, sending reporters and TV crews to film a Cornish Revolution when it was just the name of a shop, but it got them recognition and a little bit of fame. The Outrigger was a success but very hard work – everyone loved to eat there, and the two men kept the bonhomie of the place going until, eventually, it all became too much and they decided to go and work in London.

Owen was a major promoter of the Flower Power era in St Ives – openly wearing brightly flowered shirts and garlands of Heather's paper flowers around his neck and in his blonde curly hair – he was good fun and people followed his trend. Owen's partner, Rob Brown, was far more serious than his friend. Tall and lanky, with a mop of straight, blondish hair, Rob was gentle and not one bit flamboyant. He had taken great seriousness into collecting pottery – studio pottery from the likes of Bernard Leach, Janet Leach, Lucie Rie and Hans Coper, and lots of others. It became an obsession, but in the end, he had a fine collection. I last saw Rob and Owen in London when I stayed in their flat in Palace Garden Terrace, Kensington, circa 1973. I have heard that Owen passed away some years ago.

Wilhelmina Barnes-Graham became a good friend. She often invited me to her three-storey home at Barnaloft, on Porthmeor Beach. It was hard for me to think of her as the great artist that she was. Born 8th June 1912, St Andrews, Fife, Scotland, Willie was to me the epitome of a Scottish housewife with her shock of white hair, her short, stocky figure and enquiring eyes set behind spectacles. I imagined her in a country kitchen making Clootie dumpling, and not one of the foremost British abstract artists and a member of the Penwith Society of Arts. Of course, this was the Willie of the 1960s and was in her mid-fifties at this time. She was a big part of the art colony and much admired, although she could be abrupt at times. For me, her paintings were vibrant and superb – Wilhelmina Barnes-Graham will be forever immortalised in the Tate St Ives Museum. She died on 26th January 2004.

***

Born Betty Mary Newsinger on 16th February 1944 near Oxford Circus, London, she spent most of her life in West Cornwall, firstly in St Ives and then later for many years in Hayle. She changed her name to Thatcher somewhere along the line, for reasons known only to her. Although very much a Londoner, Cornwall and its landscape were to be a great inspiration to Betty as a writer, so much so that she was once described in the Melody Maker as "the Cornish Poet Betty Thatcher."

In 1972, in a strange quirk of fate, she married Rob Brown at Kensington Registry Office in London. The new Mrs Brown took it upon herself to inform me that it was merely a marriage of convenience and explained the reasons why. They divorced in 1976. Betty changed her name back to Newsinger in early 1980 when the name Thatcher gained political significance. She gained a name and recognition once she teamed up with the folk-rock band 'Renaissance' and became the 'sixth' member. During this period with 'Renaissance', Betty lost her voice due to a complete breakdown after a long-term relationship came to an end – she would not speak again for six years. But she did turn to her computer and put her thoughts to verse, and the result was a music album, produced as a CD, with ten songs that explore the ups and downs, highs and lows of love.

Betty made a complete recovery and heard her songs promoted on national and international radio stations during the following weeks. She also wrote some interesting and amusing articles and letters for the Peninsula Voice, a local paper based in Penzance. In 1978 the song 'Northern Lights' performed by Annie Haslam and the rock band 'Renaissance', from their album 'A Song For All Seasons' reached No.10 in the UK singles chart. Sadly on 15th August 2011, Betty passed away at home in Hayle after a long illness – she was 67 years old.

***

Tony O' Malley did marry his lovely Canadian girlfriend, Jane Harris, in 1973, whose influence included many winter visits to her family in the Bahamas between 1974 and 1978. These trips had an important impact on Tony's work. The escapes to a sub-tropical paradise liberated his palette. He was an artist who responded immediately to the differing environments he encountered.

O'Malley's final years were spent at Physicianstown, Callan, near his birthplace. In 1993, the Irish president Mary Robinson conferred on him the highest honour of Aosdana (the Irish body which honours writers, musicians, and artists) – the status of Saoi; and in the following year, he was awarded an honorary doctorate by Trinity College, Dublin. He died at Physicianstown, Co Kilkenny 20th January 2003, aged 90. His St Ives legacy is forever in the Tate St Ives Museum.

***

Swinging Out Into The Void – The Art of Roger Hilton – thought to be one of the best and most adventurous painters of his generation, and one of the pioneers of abstract art in post-war Britain. His paintings can be as rumbustious as the life he led. However abstract they became, the human body was never far away. During the last period of his working life, Roger returned to the childlike subjects of animals, boats, and nudes that had characterised his early work, using cheap post paints and children's brushes. Hilton deliberately approached his art with a childlike freshness of vision, but one that marked a lifetime's experience. He died at Botallack, near St Ives, in 1975. He was 64 years old. His artwork stands proudly in the Tate St Ives Museum.

***

Visiting John Milne several times at Trewyn after leaving St Ives, it became quite clear that he was not a happy man during those early 1970s. He was still represented by Marjorie Parr Gallery, both in St Ives and Chelsea. In fact, it was at the opening of a one-man exhibition at the Chelsea Gallery that I last saw John and the warning signs were very evident then. I knew he was drinking quite heavily and had put on weight – which for

John was unthinkable, but something else was amiss that I could not put my finger on. He was the star of the show at the Marjorie Parr Gallery that evening, but somehow he just wasn't there. John had always been restless and often depressive, travelling to his beloved North Africa, where good friends had a sumptuous home near Marrakesh. His constant travels to North Africa, the Middle East, and the Mediterranean seemed to me to be taking precedence over creating new sculptures, and becoming as great a sculptor as that of his much-revered friend, Barbara Hepworth.

I was staying with John at Trewyn whilst on a visit to St Ives in 1975 when the tragic fire broke out one evening at Barbara Hepworth's Trewyn studio where she lived. Barbara lost her life in that fateful fire, leaving her family, friends, the entire St Ives art colony – of which she was the stalwart, and the community of St Ives itself in complete shock and disbelief. The death of his friend and neighbour whom he had worked for and, in later years, worked with – had a profound effect on John and I truly believe he never got over it. John Milne's memorial to Barbara Hepworth, Megalith II, is the only non-Hepworth publicly sited sculpture in St Ives, aptly placed in Trewyn Gardens opposite both artists' homes. It did not come as a surprise to hear from Boots Redgrave of the death of John in St Ives in 1978 aged 46, it was just three years after that of Barbara Hepworth.

***

My brief friendship with Janet Leach did not materialise further after I moved to Heather Cottage. She was not happy about my relationship with Boots, and made it obviously clear, especially to Boots. Other than having mutual friends in Norman Stocker and John, our paths hardly crossed. In 1962, Bernard had moved to his own flat at Barnaloft, leaving Janet to run the pottery. She remained in the studio flat above the Pottery in Higher Stennack. The Newcraftsman was becoming a successful shop and gallery under the hands of Boots and the manager, Michael Hunt. Janet was a fine potter in her own right without the influence of Bernard; her pots were well sought after and commanded a high price as collector's pieces. When Bernard died in 1979, production of Leach standard ware ended, and Janet shared the pottery with Trevor Corser, an ex-apprentice, until her death in St Ives on 12th September 1997. She was 79.

***

The Newcraftsman is the oldest established Art Gallery and Craft shop in St Ives. Established in 1962, by Janet Leach, and joined later by Boots Redgrave, this gallery displays for sale, local artworks in a variety of media. Under new ownership, since the demise of both founders, today, Michael Hunt, after 55 years, retired earlier this year. It remains a beautiful shop and gallery.

***

Alas, Porthmeor Road is bereft of the iconic Mr Peggotty's, the charismatic discotheque that opened in St Ives in the mid-1960s and became the life and soul of many for years to follow. The first of its kind in the centre of the town, Peggotty's brought a new following for people – a place where you could dance the night away to disco music with disco lights and a floor full of people. It closed in 1998, and Porthmeor Road has never been the same. Holiday flats adorn the once revered premises and look as lifeless as a dead fish. Where have all the Flowers Gone?

The Sugar 'n' Spice, in St Andrews Street, The Blue Haven, St Andrews Street, and The Cortina Café, in The Warren, are no longer in existence. The premises remain, but they could be a zillion light years away from what they once were, hustling and bustling cafés alive with people, full of atmosphere as guitar music, mouth organ playing, and song rang out of doors and windows as life entered in and out, or you were just walking past. All gone now, all rather sad.

***

Oh, for the joy of seeing St Ives Arts Club on Westcott's Quay very much open, up and running. Visual arts. Performing arts. Exhibitions. Live music and theatre. What a little gem this place is. A few years ago, a fierce storm ravaged Westcott's Quay, with waves smashing against the Arts Club building, causing extensive damage. A mass of scaffolding was needed for the repairs to take place as well as a lot of money. Today, the work is complete, and the Arts Club is back in place with its ongoing art exhibitions and Café Frug, on Thursday evenings, in the upstairs theatre, showcasing a variety of eclectic performances from local artists, poets, musicians, and writers.

St Ives Arts Cub has been in operation since its founding year in 1890. Membership, originally restricted to professional artists, musicians, and authors has been widened over the years to include, for example, drama, photography, comedy, and even those with simply a keen interest in the arts.

***

After leaving Cornwall, I found breaking the tie difficult and would try and visit whenever possible, staying either at Trewyn or with Boots at Heather Cottage. On occasions, Boots would come to London, sometimes on a business trip with Janet, or by herself for a break to see family and friends. We often had dinner at L'Artiste Assoiffe, not far from where I was living, and a restaurant that Boots enjoyed and approved of. One memorable evening, when we were in this lovely restaurant, which was pretty full, we were asked by the maître d' if we minded changing tables from the four-seater we were sitting at, to a two-seater as they had four people waiting. Of course, we didn't mind in the slightest as the maître d' had asked so charmingly. At the end of the meal, the waiter brought us each a glass of Remy Martin and an espresso coffee which we hadn't ordered – it was "on the house," he said, seeing our surprise. This was indeed a lovely end to a special evening, as we enjoyed our cognac and coffee which more than made up for changing tables. When we finally asked for the 'bill' we were told that our evening at L'Artiste Assoiffe, was all 'on the house'. What a wonderful and generous gesture that was!

My visits to Cornwall became less and less over the following years, and when John died in 1978, they became even less. Boots was deeply embedded with her partnership in the Newcraftsman, improving the gallery from year to year. She had an exceptionally 'good eye' for spotting talented artists, potters, and jewellers to display their work in the gallery, and with the help of Michael Hunt, they made the Newcraftsman the superb gallery and shop that it became. In 2008 the gallery eventually changed hands after the death of Mary 'Boots' Redgrave in May 2002. She was 79. The present owners maintain an equally high standard in the Newcraftsman today that 'Boots' would be proud of.

***

The former public schoolboy, Arthur Caddick, once revered as 'The Poet Laureate of Cornwall', writer, poet, charmer, and hell-raiser lived for thirty-six years in the same cottage 'Windswept', with his wife, Peggy and their five children up above the village of Nancledra. It's where he found the inspiration he was searching for. In the following poem (in part), Arthur paid homage to the county and its people that had been his lifeblood for so many years.

Valedictory

One should say thank you before taking leave
Of a host who is half-a-lifetime's friend.
Only the uncouth would neglect this.
So, for prudence sake let me now give thanks
For all that Cornwall has meant to me and mine.

It kept my children younger than their years,
Still innocent when city children were not.
It made their growing bodies strong, as they trudged
Uphill and down, through rain and gales and heat.
To their village school, that gentle stage
Which eased their transit to a harder world.
And their mother trudged beside them, between
Her tasks at home, to keep them safe on roads,
And my love went with her always.

As for me my long legs strode for twenty years
Over croft, up granite slopes, down to coves,
As I watched the quick-change light and scented
Heath, furze, bracken, wild thyme, earth-thralled
Things,
While the wind sang to those, who walk alone.
I always used a stick I cut myself,
Oak, blackthorn, ash, holly, hazel, hawthorn,
And, in the terms of trade of the forgetful,
I mostly lost them, at inns, or where you will.
I have embellished this peninsula with fifteen
Fathoms of polished dead branches.
Instinct led me from London to Penzance.

Arthur Bruce Caddick – died 1987. He lies beside his ever-patient wife Peggy, in his beloved Cornwall.

***

Arriving in St Ives in the early 1960s from the

Midlands, Brian Smith, worked for a while at the Newcraftsman shop that Janet Leach established in Fore Street. It was Janet who recommended Brian to her friend Barbara Hepworth, when Barbara needed a personal assistant, prior to the big Tate retrospective exhibition of her sculpture in 1968. After Barbara's death in 1975, the family and trustees followed her wishes and made the studio and garden at Trewyn into a small private museum. Brian proved to be the museum's ideal custodian. When the trustees gave the Barbara Hepworth Museum to the nation to be managed by the Tate Gallery, this was the beginning of the Tate's involvement in St Ives.

Brian and his team now worked for the Tate, and Brian continued to serve as the curator of the Hepworth Museum until he retired in 1992. In gratitude for the help he had given her, Barbara bequeathed Brian the cottage in Barnoon Hill, where he lived for the remainder of his life.

Remembering Brian in those halcyon days of 'al fresco' lunches on the lawn at Trewyn, nearly every day – weather permitting, during his lunch hour and ours – brings joy to mind as he was indeed the wittiest person imaginable with a wicked sense of humour. How we laughed through those lunches. Brian was a good friend to John, and we all loved him, even Ivaldo. Brian died in Turkey in 2004, he was 71.

***

Marjorie Parr founded her original gallery at 285 Kings Road, Chelsea (now a shoe, dress and accessories shop) in 1963. In May 1968, the success of her London Gallery prompted her to buy a property in Wills Lane, St Ives. In 1971, after what appeared to be a successful time in St Ives, Marjorie Parr sold her Will's Lane gallery. The reasons are not known, and even Peter Davies' fine biography on Parr does not make it clear.

Marjorie sold her Kings Road Gallery to David Gilbert in July 1974 but continued to assist him at the gallery until the end of 1975. Gilbert renamed the gallery in March 1977 to the Gilbert Parr Gallery and continued to trade successfully until he finally closed it in October 1982. Marjorie died on May 27th 2007, in her 101st year.

***

Carol and I last saw the infamous Colin Pryor in a café on the Hayle bypass before he scooped off to Ibiza with a load of money he and his partner had fraudulently acquired by setting up as Estate Agents and applying for mortgages for fictitious people. Colin built up a successful sports centre in Ibiza, but sadly he died there in his 40's – I believe with an undetected heart problem. His partner in crime, known as JD, voluntarily came back to the UK and was arrested as he got off the plane. He received quite a long sentence which he knew he would get.

***

Bryan Herbert Wynter died 2nd February 1975, aged 60. I saw his gravestone in the little churchyard of St Senara in Zennor. It saddened me to see this more than I could say. Bryan was a lovely man (1958), a great artist, and so much part of the St Ives art scene through the '60s and '70s. An auction record for his painting In the Streams Path (1958) is £131,000, set at Sotheby's on 11 November 2016. The work had been acquired by the pop star David Bowie at the sale of the collection of Sir John Moores.

In 2001 he was the subject of Bryan Wynter: A Selected Retrospective at Tate St Ives. I'm happy to know that Bryan's work hangs in the Tate St Ives Museum.

***

I have visited the fishermen from time to time at Shamrock, Rose, and Shore Shelters. There is little activity and I bump into the odd fisherman now and then, but nobody knows Seth, and I don't recognise any of my friends from the '60s. It is hard to forget that they were probably a lot older than I was then, and are no longer alive. The shelters themselves still stand in what must be the prime position on St Ives harbourfront. Certainly still used though an air of – being out of place surrounds them, with the glittering tourist shops, cafés, ice cream parlours, and a humming throng spread about outside the Sloop Inn. But I love these shelters and wish I could turn back the clock fifty-five years. To find myself huddled around a warm black stove burning in the middle of the shelter, with the smell of pipe and cigarette tobacco permeating the room as a storm lashes outside. And drinking tea while listening to the stories and yarns from those craggy-faced fishermen.

Chapter Twelve

Where The Light Is

When I left St Ives in the early '70s, with a lift to London from Sally and Sandy, I had no idea, no clue, and no plan whatsoever of what I was going to do other than trying to make something out of the time I spent in St Ives learning to become a jeweller. A real thrust into the unknown, as I didn't know London, apart from a couple of brief weekends I spent there, or in fact, anybody who lived there only Rob and Owen, at least I could now add Sally and Sandy to the list.

Arriving in London was a whole new life away from St Ives and Cornwall. Knowing that there was no going back made me feel like a ship lost at sea, floundering in an unknown ocean. Sally's flat was in Elgin Crescent, near Portobello Road, and it was lovely. Situated on the first floor of a large Victorian House – that I discovered belonged to Sandy's parents - the flat was large, airy and comfortable, and the two girls at once, made me feel at home. On the first night, Sandy produced an enormous salad which we ate with cheeses, baked potatoes and a nice bottle of wine – it was heavenly, and that night I slept like never before.

The following days, Sally gave me quick tours around the area, including the famous Portobello Road, Notting Hill Gate, Bayswater Road, Holland Park Avenue, and Kensington. Getting petrol at a garage around the corner from Elgin Crescent, I saw we were in Blenheim Crescent, which rang a bell, then remembered that Nicola Wood, who has stayed at Trewyn with Father Brocard Sewell, had given me her address and it was Blenheim Crescent. Not only that, but her studio literally backed onto the house where I was staying.

After a few days with Sally, I moved into Rob and

Owen's basement flat in Palace Gardens Terrace, Kensington. They gave me a sofa to sleep on, and an area under the stairs big enough to make a small jewellery workbench, to set out my tools – it was perfect for a while until something more permanent presented itself. As Bryan Illsley had suggested, I made an appointment to see the Curator at Goldsmith Hall to ask his advice about jewellery making, working as an assistant-jobbing jeweller for one of the jewellery workshops in Hatton Garden. The curator in the hallowed halls of Goldsmiths' shunned this idea immediately, and suggested that I start up on my own, and not to waste time in somebody else's workshop where I'd be used and get nowhere. Wise advice indeed, but it didn't feel like it then.

Owen was working at the Bacchus wine shop in Kensington Church Street, and one early evening, I was passing by the shop and dropped in to say hello, and to buy a bottle of wine. He was pleased to see me and introduced me to a customer he was chatting to whose name was Flo, a nearby neighbour in Palace Garden Terrace. We exchanged pleasantries, and she ended up inviting Rob, Owen and myself for dinner to her and her boyfriend, John's flat, a couple of evenings later, which turned out to be a small dinner party. It was at this dinner party, along with other guests, a lady named Anthea, mentioned that the writer, Elizabeth Sprigg, was looking for a part-time housekeeper-cum-assistant and there could be a flat thrown in with the job – it was only a five minute walk away in Ladbroke Grove, and suggested I apply for it.

A few days later I found myself on the doorstep of a four-storey house on top of the rise in Ladbroke Grove, pressing the doorbell and waiting with bated breath. After what seemed an interminable time, the door was eventually opened and the kindly lady who opened it introduced herself as Priaulx Rainier. Feeling pretty dumbfounded to find myself face to face with the reclusive composer, I was at a loss for words – with a name like that there couldn't be two – this had to be her, the one person in St Ives that had eluded me. Priaulx was charming, friendly, and a joy to talk to. She told me she had a large studio-apartment on the first floor of the house that was once used by the opera singer, Enrico Caruso.

Elizabeth Sprigg gave me the job, and a large basement flat to go with it. She owned the entire house and had the ground floor herself. She let apartments out to Priaulx and her sister, Nella, an artist, Peter Lloyd-Jones, and one of her granddaughters. The basement flat was unfurnished and enormous with its own entrance at the front as well as into the house at the top of some stairs. I was to keep an eye on the house, sort out the post, cook the odd meal, and drive Elizabeth to visit friends and keep appointments. I was allowed to use the car myself on occasions should the need arise. To have fallen with my bum in the butter once again, was an understatement.

From that moment on, I felt settled in London. I scrubbed that basement flat from top to bottom – hosing down the flagstone floors, scrubbing away the grime and paint where necessary until it shone. Beg, borrowed and stole furniture from the outside skips from houses being renovated, borrowed a couple of Peter Lloyd-Jones's massive canvases to put on the walls. Made half the kitchen into a workroom and hey presto! I was in business.

The flat was situated in short distances between John and Flo, Rob and Owen, and Sally and Sandy, which meant that I had friends on the doorstep, and we met often, dined at the flat frequently, and enjoyed each other's company when we could, especially at weekends. After a long slog and much hard work, I did break into the jewellery trade, with exhibitions at the Design Centre in the Haymarket, London, Amalgam Gallery in Barnes, Liberty's of London, and eventually with my own shop at the bottom of Ladbroke Grove, off Holland Park Avenue, which I also lived above. My jewellery became sought after, the shop was successful and I'd achieved what I had set out from St Ives to do.

Priaulx and I, by this time, had become good friends.

She was professional and totally dedicated to her work, composing every day at the grand piano in her studio. We often had a drink together in the evening between 5-7 p.m., which were moments that I treasured. Sitting in Priaulx's studio was a privilege, surrounded by paintings given to her by her dear friend, Ben Nicholson, whom she admired greatly, and music scores sitting on top of the piano, written for Yehudi Menuhin. *What greatness she surrounded herself with*, I used to think, munching on the large black-oily olives that Priaulx always produced. The studio looked out over the beautiful garden below which she drew inspiration from. She told me of the compensation she received from a motor accident that enabled her to buy 'Tregenna Steps Studio', in St Ives. This was her own, where she went to compose in silence and solitude. After drinks, she would go to join her sister Nella for supper, in her apartment on the floor above.

A passionate gardener and ecologist, who helped design and plant the exotic shrubs in Barbara Hepworth's Sculpture Garden in St Ives. Priaulx loved to visit the Isabella Plantation in Richmond Park, a 40-acre woodland garden set within a Victorian plantation in the 1830s. This was 'our' place, a place where Priaulx, Nella, and I would, as often as time allowed, take a picnic to enjoy in Isabella Plantation, surrounded by nature's beauty and wildlife, where azaleas, rhododendrons, and camellias grow in profusion. A beautiful place to escape to, and a short drive out of London.

It was 1977 and The Promenade Concert season at the Royal Albert Hall has started. Yehudi Menuhin will be performing Priaulx Rainiers' 'Due canti e finale', a violin concerto, commissioned by him, and will be first performed at one of the concerts. Priaulx has invited me to The Proms for this performance. I'm beside myself with pride for this living composer, one of the gentlest and most humble people I have ever met who, at 74 years old, has achieved such greatness in the world of classical music.

Ivy Priaulx Rainier was born in Howick, Natal,

South Africa, on 3rd February 1903. She had two older sisters, Ellen (Nella) and Eveline, both played the piano, whereas Priaulx took more naturally to the violin. When the family moved to Cape Town in 1913, Priaulx attended the college of music and developed an interest in string quartet playing. In 1919, she received a bursary from the University of the Cape of Good Hope that enabled her to continue her studies at the Royal Academy of Music (RAM) in London. In 1939, she was appointed a Professor of Composition at RAM.

In June 1982, she was awarded a Doctorate of Music (Honoris Causa) by the University of Cape Town, where her scores are now housed. In 1986, on a visit to France, Priaulx passed away at Besse-en-Chandesse, aged 83.

Discovering Nicola Wood was living back-to-back with Sally in Elgin Crescent, I got in touch with her. Her studio was pretty impressive – only one of two in Blenheim Crescent – it spanned the entire house from top to bottom with a mezzanine floor made into a bedroom. I spent some happy hours in that studio drinking tea and chatting to Nicola's dad when he was visiting from up north. This connection with Nicola brought me in touch with Father Brocard Sewell again, and we became firm friends over the following years. Brocard was based with the Carmelite Order at Aylesford Priory during this time and invited me to visit on several occasions, staying for long weekends when I would have supper at the long refectory tables with the rest of the friars. The food was simple but always delicious, and wine was served for those who wanted it.

In the Winter, there would be a huge crackling fire burning in the dining hall, sending out a warm glow, giving the feeling of being at a medieval banquet. After supper, Brocard and I would go into the library and have coffee while discussing many subjects including Christine Keeler, Henry Williamson and Brocard's controversial letter that he wrote to The Times in 1968 protesting at the papal report on birth control. Being with Brocard amongst the Carmelite's gave me a sense of peace that I needed during that period of my life.

Father Brocard (Michael) Sewell, priest, printer, writer, and scholar, theologian, and a brilliant connoisseur of the 1890s decadence. This small owlish man with a quizzical but imperturbable expression, was an unforgettable figure on the fringes of English literary life, born 30th July 1912; died 2nd April 2000 aged 88.

It was a nice surprise to get a phone call from Galina von Meck one day, shortly after arriving in London. She'd heard from Bertie Pocock, via John, that I had moved from St Ives, and suggested we meet. She was in Richmond, and I joined her for lunch in her small apartment there. Being alone in the presence of Tchaikovsky's grand-niece felt awesome. At Trewyn, she was always with Bertie or someone, and I never got the chance to have a proper conversation with her. Now there I was, sitting at her table, in a room surrounded by papers, books and all things pertaining to the writer. Galina looked the aristocratic Russian that she was. The apartment felt Russian. Galina, probably aged 84 at the time, had surrounded herself with the familiarity of her ancestry. Once again, I felt privileged to have met someone as interesting as this noble lady. We met a couple of times after that, and I never saw her again. Galina Nikolayevna von Meck – Born 12th October 1891 – Died 9th April 1985 aged 93.

Glyn Vaughan, the beautiful surfer, who captivated my heart so long ago – eventually left Cornwall to be reunited with his family in Australia where he later died. His guardian and friend, Jim Prentice, was once the owner of The Porthminster Hotel, together with Geraldine. After The Porthminster, the three of them went to 'The Rashleigh Arms' in Polkerris, near Fowey, which they owned or just managed. From there, Jim and Geraldine have eluded me. Jim's spiritual home was always Spain. Retirement there would seem appropriate. Perhaps the same has happened to John Jones and Bill Watson – flourishing in Spain somewhere – last heard of in Ibiza and

Majorca.

Sally Hall, who drove me from Cornwall to London to start a new life, eventually packed her old Mercedes car, her black Labrador Zac, and herself, onto a cargo ship and sailed across to Argentina. Heartbroken friends followed her journey through Patagonia via her mother, Lola Hall, with whom we spent happy weekends at her home in Sussex, catching up on travels with Sally. After travelling some dodgy months through Patagonia, Sally got the news that her uncle Don, living in Majorca, had died, and his wife, Rosita, was left bereft and not knowing what to do. Sally immediately made elaborate plans to get to Majorca taking Zac with her. Sally remained in Majorca for some years and even purchased a small finca (farm) there. Being in Majorca, meant that we, her friends, could now visit Sally – being a lot nearer than South America. Lola was delighted to have her daughter nearer, and she too spent time on the island.

After an unpleasant divorce from her QC husband, Lola decided to move from Sussex to South Africa. A few years after, Sally wanted to do the same and getting on a Greek cargo ship in Lisbon with her beloved Zac, sailed to Cape Town to join her mother. Three days after arriving in Cape Town in 1981, Sally joined a Montessori School teaching primary children. Some months later, she wanted to be able to teach children of all races, but this was during the apartheid regime in South Africa and was not allowed. Sally made the decision to start her own school, which she did in a residential area of Cape Town – it was a long haul to establish after finding a large, attractive Victorian House to use as a school. It was the first school in South Africa to have pupils of mixed race – a brave thing to do against the apartheid establishment in those days. Sally persevered, and when Nelson Mandela was inaugurated as the country's first black president on May 10, 1994, the school applied for registration with the Department of Education and received a resounding accolade when the school inspectors came to review the school.

Thirty-six years later, the school is the leading Montessori School in the country. It has grown in enormous proportions, the education is excellent, and Sally has been an outstanding Principal, much loved and admired by both staff and pupils. Today, forty-nine years later, Sally remains my best and closest friend. Her mother Lola, passed away this year, she was 100 years old.

My brother, Geoff, on a visit to London, pointed out a large vertical crack in the building housing the jewellery shop and my home. This was a row of five shops, including a post office. We contacted the owner of the property immediately, who lived around the corner in Holland Park Avenue, and without hesitation, she sent a property surveyor to check the building. The crack was in the middle of the row through the shop and the two-storey flat above. It was going to be a massive job having to pin the building back, affecting the entire row. When the work started some months later, I decided to move out and went to live in a cottage I shared in Hampshire. The repairs took forever. Making visits periodically to see how things were getting on, I found that the builders were sleeping in the flat, things went missing, and I could see that there would be need of complete re-decoration of the shop and flat before moving back. Getting more and more dejected by the entire process (and still paying rent), I decided to sell the leasehold and call it a day.

This was a big turning point. There was no longer any need to be in London, Hampshire had no particular calling, but the yearning to return to Cornwall was forever present. The dream of one day owning a cottage in Zennor presented itself on a quick visit there in 1983. Before lunch at the Tinner's Arms with my friend, Susan, we were walking past Post Office row, a row of cottages just behind St Senara Church, when a young man came out of one of the doors, and I asked him about properties in Zennor. Very much to our surprise, he told us that he and his wife were selling the cottage next door pointing to a much smaller house beside the one he was coming out of. My heart sang, bells whistled, he showed us there and then the inside of the cottage, told us the price they were asking, we negotiated, agreed on a price, shook hands, went back to the Tinner's, and enjoyed a ploughman's lunch. All done within half an hour, and we were on the road to becoming the proud owners of 'Winifred's Cottage' in Zennor.

Being back in Cornwall and living in Zennor was a different place altogether than it was living in St Ives twelve years earlier. Summers were sometimes good, but on the whole, it was wet, cold, damp and shrouded in mist. We loved the cottage and enjoyed the small garden. We took long walks to Zennor Head and the cliffs, exploring the surrounding countryside. Susan worked at the Tinner's during the day, on occasions, and for a local family helping out with their five children. I opened a tack shop in Penzance. We each bought a horse from local farmers and rode over the moors. For me, this was the highlight of being in Zennor, discovering, and seeing everything on horseback – how we loved those times. Strangely, I hardly ever went to St Ives, apart from going to the Chinese Restaurant on the Wharf – usually with a group from Zennor. I saw Boots occasionally, but something was gone that I couldn't put my finger on.

We were included in the Zennor community and enjoyed mixing with the locals, and being part of the village. The Count House at Botallack since I was last there, had changed hands and become a first-class restaurant owned by the Long family. Anne Long was a chef par excellence producing the very best in cuisine, while her husband, Ian, did 'front of house'. It was hard, not to go to the Count House – even in the bleakest of winter and way off the beaten track, it was always fully booked. This special restaurant, being a firm favourite, kept us working hard to be able to eat there.

In 1978, an opportunity had presented itself for me to visit South Africa. My sister Brenda, and her family were now living there permanently, and I longed to see them. Leaving freezing conditions in February and flying into the warm sunshine which greeted me in Cape Town was wonderful. Time spent with my sister and brother-in-law, my niece and two nephews was very special. Lola, Sally's mum, was now settled in Cape Town and loving her life there – we spent a couple of happy days together and talked nonstop. Returning to England at the end of March left me feeling low and despondent.

Going back to Cornwall, I realised, had not been the right thing to do. Time had moved on and somewhere in the back of my psyche, it was not where I wanted to be. I was standing on the top of the rocks at Zennor head one day, looking out across the Atlantic Ocean and thinking *'how long it would take to sail to South Africa if a yacht happened to pass'* (a yacht was found floating helmless in the cove below Tregarthen weeks before), and I knew at that moment, South Africa was where I wanted to be.

The plane touched down in Johannesburg on 13th April 1987. Brenda and Neville were living in Swaziland for a couple of years, as Neville was working on a contract there. So off I flew to Swaziland for a few weeks, staying with them and exploring the small kingdom. We visited the Kruger National Park, I loved it, seeing the abundance of wild animals to me, was breath-taking, that and the sheer size of the Kruger Park (the size of Wales).

Having explored Swaziland and a great deal of the Eastern Transvaal, while I was in the North, it was Cape Town that attracted me the most. I moved to Cape Town, found a lovely flat overlooking the yacht harbour in Simon's Town, and settled in. Sally, now living in another area of Cape Town, offered me a part-time position in the finance office at her school, where I stayed for the next twelve years. On the spur of the moment, I bought a small sailing boat and learned to sail. Then attempted to do yacht racing, and finally won races. Becoming the first female 'Commodore' of FBYC on the Cape Peninsula after fifty years of male dominance – was the proudest moment of my life.

These days, Wildlife Conservation is close to my

heart. I spent three years in Kenya, a place where I belong, being connected to wildlife through lions and elephant, in particular, working in places such as the Masai Mara (the great migration) head-counting lions. Amboseli, head-counting elephant – has been one of the greatest experiences that I could ever have imagined. Today, I am the Chairman of 'Wild Rescue' – Wildlife Sanctuary and Nature Reserve', based in the Western Cape.

Our destinies are chosen, and I was never meant to return to Cornwall in 1983. My darling mother told me before she died (I was twelve years old), that I should travel and see the world, and not be pressurised into getting married and having children until I had seen and experienced something of life. Wise words from a wonderful woman, and that's what I have done.

Now I am back in Cornwall to finish this book, and it feels absolutely right. Sadly, there is little left of the once close art community, or the diminishing fishing industry of the 1960s. The vibrancy and the intimacy that once captivated and united us has been sucked out of the town. The hubs of our existence, The Sloop, The Castle, The Golden Lion, The Lifeboat and The Arts Club, no longer smell or feel familiar, and why should they? St Andrews Street does not buzz with The Sugar 'n' Spice and The Blue Haven's open doors belting out the music of Donovan, Gypsy Dave, and other musicians singing and strumming guitars. Brenda Wootton was Cornwall, and it saddens me we shall never hear her singing here again.

Robert Short and Seth no longer hang around the harbour with their easy swagger, as I know not where they are. Fish Street, Downalong, Back Road East and West, Porthmeor Road, Carncrows Road are no longer alive, the locals have sold out – and who can blame them – to people prepared to pay high prices and turn them into holiday homes for letting. In winter, the entire Downalong area is quiet, no lights or twitching curtains, no friendly waves, no dogs, no cats or a natter on the doorstep. Even Porthmeor Studios and the surrounding areas, where once you'd see artists in and out of each other's studios or dropping into the Penwith Gallery, now appear lifeless. Studios which once opened onto the beach I've passed, but not a soul or a canvas or easel in sight.

But we are in 2019, and of course things have changed for better or worse – depending on how you view them! Tourism has reached an all-time zenith, and there is no doubt this has been perpetuated by the arrival of the mighty Tate St Ives Museum in 1993. It now receives 210,000 visitors each year. It has won the Art Fund 'Museum of the Year' and £100,000 in 2018, the largest and most prestigious museum prize in the world, and is being lauded as 'One of Britain's most Beautiful Galleries' by The Telegraph. After receiving this great announcement, banners were hung in celebration across Fore Street and heralded on the front of the museum. Knowing little of The Tate Museum when I visited St Ives in 2018, made it a perfect time to see for myself what the phenomenon was that had been built on the site of the once familiar gas works.

Nothing could have prepared me! Painting after painting by my old friends, Tony O'Malley, Bryan Pearce, Roger Hilton, Patrick Heron, Willie Barnes-Graham, Bryan Wynter, John Miller – sculptures of John Milne, Barbara Hepworth and Denis Mitchell and the pottery of Bernard and Janet Leach. They were all there, so much part of the past, and now so much part of the present and of the future. I am proud to have known these artists, to know what they went through to get there. The agonies and the ecstasy, poor one day, rich the next, if you happened to sell a painting that put bread on the table. Some struggled, others didn't, but that's the life of an artist. Now their work is in the Tate St Ives Museum, immortalised forever and priceless. Thank you, Mr Sugarman!

Lightning Source UK Ltd.
Milton Keynes UK
UKHW040636141222
413914UK00004B/410

9 781789 557701